ZEL

MARKOVIC MMA

Roxie Rivera

Night Works Books
College Station, Texas

CHAPTER ONE

BORED BEYOND BELIEF, Zel Tesla dragged his gaze away from the gyrating, whip-cracking dancer entertaining the room. Heady cigar smoke melded with the faint aromas of aged rums and cognacs in the VIP room of Las Vegas' hottest gentleman's club. An invitation-only crowd of promoters, agents, fighters and hangers-on packed the darkened space.

A flash of movement off to the left caught his waning attention. He glanced that way just in time to see Erin Markovic slide out of her chair and right onto her husband's lap. From the surprised expression on Ivan's hard face, he hadn't expected his wife to behave so brazenly. Judging by her flushed smile, Erin had had a little too much champagne tonight and didn't really care who saw her cozying up to her husband.

But Ivan didn't seem to mind his wife perching on his lap like a naughty little kitten. He wound his muscular arms around the willowy beauty and kissed the side of her neck. Laughing, Erin leaned into her husband's embrace. He nuzzled her neck and dotted a line of kisses along the curve of her throat. She captured his heavily tattooed hand in her thinner, elegant one and threaded their fingers together.

They were an oddly mismatched couple, like Beauty and her Beast, but they were the happiest pair Zel had ever known.

Tonight, they seemed particularly pleased with one another. Watching the erotic show unfold onstage appeared to be quite the aphrodisiac for the couple.

Ivan's massive hand spanned Erin's slim waist and he pulled her back against him. He whispered something in her ear, and she bit her lower lip before turning to nod enthusiastically at her husband. Ivan reached into his jacket and retrieved a money clip. He peeled off a thick stack of cash and dropped it next to his barely touched drink.

Giving Erin's hip a pat, he said something to her that made her blush. In the next instant, she stood up and tugging on his hand, dragging him out of his chair. When he was on his feet, Ivan grasped her hand and took charge, leading her out of the shadowy VIP area with purposeful strides.

Not wanting to get caught watching his coach seduce his wife, Zel returned to his attention to the stage, but his gaze didn't linger there long. Still not entertained by the show, he turned his gaze to the right side of the room. A little farther down, Mace McCoy, his soon-to-be opponent, relaxed in his chair and sipped a glass of ice water. This close to a fight every calorie counted. It was about fuel and stamina at this point. A sip of alcohol could throw their bodies off-balance and leave them struggling in the cage.

Stocky and heavily muscled, Mace had always reminded Zel of a bulldog. He even had the pronounced lower jaw and under-bite. Their eyes met briefly across the darkness. Even in the friendly atmosphere of the arranged get-together, the spark of aggressiveness and competition reared its head. For the first time in quite a while, Zel was actually looking forward to a fight. Worthy opponents were few and far between in his weight class.

Zel's gaze returned to the performer on the low dais at the front of the room. Dressed like a Gothic pixie, the young woman in shiny black latex panties and side-lacing red stiletto thigh-high boots danced seductively and swung her whip. Brittle streaks of red wax clung to her perky breasts. Dark angelic tattoos curled around her thin arms and wrapped around both sides of her neck. She brought visions of flogging and boot-licking to his mind, neither of which he found particularly sexy.

While her show appeared to enthrall the rest of the room, it did very little for Zel. These days little seemed to interest him. The other single fathers in the grief support group he secretly attended had all reported similar experiences. The married men or those with long-term partners seemed to have better luck when it came to love after losing a child.

But, then again, he'd never had much luck with love.

Since becoming a single father just days after his son was born until the day he had lost his boy, Zel had had no successful relationships with women. There had been two or three women in those eight years who had managed to hold his interest for a few weeks, but he hadn't been in any kind of position to offer a woman a meaningful commitment.

He had been wholly focused on his son to the detriment of everything else in his life. He had been alone for so long he wasn't even sure he knew *how* to be part of a relationship. Now, when he most needed a connection to another human being to keep him grounded in life, he utterly lacked the skills for even a first date. He didn't have a chance in hell of ever making something like Ivan and Erin's marriage work.

The curtain fell as the Gothic pixie's dance ended. Hip-hop music filtered through the sound system, masking the sounds of the stage being struck and reset. Scantily clad waitresses roamed the room, offering alcoholic beverages and cigars. Zel dismissed a waitress by lifting his glass of ice water. Smiling understandingly, she moved along to the next patron. Wanting to see how many performers remained before he could cut out of here without making problems for Ivan with the league's PR team, Zel picked up the glossy program resting on his lap and thumbed through the pages.

Before he could find the right page, the lights dimmed and a soft, pulsing Latin beat began playing. The curtain lifted to reveal a bathroom and dressing area reminiscent of the art deco heydays of Miami. Black-and-white-checkered floor and subway tiles lent an air of realism to the set. A white clawfoot tub sat downstage, a black lacquered vanity and tufted chartreuse bench just to its right. An armoire stuffed with bright silks and satins and a dresser overflowing with lingerie rounded out the furniture props. A bottle of tequila, shot glass, saltshaker and bowl of limes decorated the dresser. Gauzy white curtains framed a false balcony and billowed in a fake breeze. Potted palms gave the scene a South Beach feel.

Brassy and bold, the salsa tune's tempo and volume increased. Finally, a colorfully costumed young woman strutted onto the stage, her ample hips swiveling side to side in perfect rhythm with her music. Enthusiastic applause greeted Nena Rubens, the world-renowned BBW burlesque.

The sight of the voluptuous beauty paralyzed Zel—he couldn't even lift his hands to clap. Enthralled, Zel swallowed hard and watched her dance.

When the stage lights fully illuminated her face, he finally recognized her as the sultry, curvaceous goddess gracing the billboard near the warehouse where he trained back in Houston. In that photograph, her shiny black hair splayed wildly about her head as she reclined against a mound of pink pillows, her luscious figure barely covered in upscale lingerie.

Tonight Nena wore a strapless hot pink gown similar to Carmen Miranda's gaudy getup. As she sensually danced toward the front of the stage, her gloved hands swished the diagonal ruffles of her lime green chiffon skirt. Because the skirt split at the top of her thighs, every swish provided the crowd with a tantalizing glimpse of caramel skin, pink garters and black stockings. She smiled mischievously and nipped the tip of a pink satin elbow-length glove. Twirling it overhead, she gave a hip-swiveling spin and tossed the glove into the crowd. She did the same with the other glove, spinning in the opposite direction this time.

She shimmied to the front of the stage and flicked through the hidden hooks keeping her dress closed. As she danced in a circle, the dress fell to the floor. She sent it stage left with a playful kick. A pink satin cincher trimmed her thick waist, and a black bra adorned with pink beads and sequins enhanced her abundant bosom.

Enthralled by her plump hourglass figure, Zel watched her sashay across the stage, her movements punctuated by the brassy trumpet notes. She made a show of pouring a tequila shot, licking the inside of her left wrist and applying salt. With a devilish smile, she swiped her tongue across the salt and kicked back the shot.

As she sucked the lime juice from the green wedge

clamped between her lips, Nena poured another shot. She placed the shot in the tight valley between her heaving breasts. Ass wiggling, she squeezed a fresh lime on the tan crest of her left breast. She sprinkled salt over the wet juice. A second lime wedge was tucked between the cup of her bra and her right breast.

Zel anxiously devoured her buxom figure as she slowly danced her way down the steps of the dais. When she reached the small patch of floor in front of the seated crowd, her eyes scanned the room.

Me. Pick me.

As if hearing his silent plea, Nena moved in his direction. Zel's stomach dropped as she stopped in front of him and winked. She gestured for him to take the shot. Throat dry and fingers trembling, he sat forward in his seat. His pulse clamored so loudly against his eardrums it drowned out the sound of music and the hooting crowd.

And the phantom boom of Ivan's angry voice when he dressed him down for drinking…

When he swiped his flattened tongue along the salted curve of her breast, their gazes locked, his cobalt eyes clashing against her chocolate orbs. Savoring the salty lime flavor, he buried his nose in her soft cleavage and wrapped his lips and teeth around the shot glass. Tilting his head back, he swallowed the burning liquid and removed the glass from his mouth. Glass in hand, he plucked the lime from her bra with his lips and squashed it between his teeth. Citrus juice trickled down his chin, and Nena, ever the temptress, trailed a fingertip along his wet skin and brought it to her mouth, sucking the juice from her finger.

Smirking sexily, Nena danced back onto the stage. Hips rocking, she squatted and gave the crowd a full view of her frilly panties. Her nimble fingers unhooked the pink cincher. Swaying side to side, Nena stood and opened the cincher, revealing a pink diamond heart dangling from a navel piercing. She flung the cincher overhead and strutted to the vanity, her black pumps elongating her strides and tightening her calves.

Sitting on the tufted bench, Nena crossed and uncrossed her legs. Zel's heart raced with each glimpse of her inner thighs. She kicked off her shoes and removed the silver clasp holding her low chignon. With a wild shake, waves of black hair tumbled down her back. She unsnapped her garters and pulled the black stocking from her right leg, bending her knee until her heel touched her thigh. She tossed the stocking into the crowd and the men fought over it.

Using the second stocking as a prop, she salsaed down to the crowd again, stretching her supple brown legs as she bobbed. She held the stocking tight against her chest and approached Pete Lazzo, the man who'd arranged tonight's entertainment. For a man who worked with some of the most physically fit athletes in the world, Pete obviously hadn't picked up any of their habits. He was a big bear of a man. His belly paunch sagged against his tailored shirt and overlapped the top of his pants. As always, he clamped a cigar between his teeth. As Nena approached, Pete snatched the unlit cigar from his mouth.

Quite the saucy minx, she looped her stocking around Pete's neck and used it to pull him close. Pete's expression was one of embarrassment as she shook her breasts in his face.

Laughing, Nena planted a kiss on his shiny bald head and danced away, leaving her stocking draped around Pete's shoulders and a bright red lip print on his head.

Back onstage, Nena dropped her garter belt and turned her back on the crowd. Hungrily, Zel and the spectators watched her unhook her bra. She faced the crowd again but kept the bra pressed to her breasts. He pulsed with a desperate craving to see more of her naked flesh but she refused to alleviate his need. She continued sassily twisting and bending. Other strippers would have been completely naked by now and writhing raunchily. That she lengthened the tease made him crave her all the more.

He fantasized about having her in his bed. God, what he would do with her! He imagined burying his face between those thick thighs or his cock sliding between her ample breasts. For the first time in so long, he ached for a woman.

The room erupted with wild whistling and hollering as Nena threw her bra into the crowd and exposed her black and hot pink nipple tassels. The music reached a crescendo as Nena jumped up and down on her toes. With every hop, her breasts jiggled wildly, the tassels whipping in fast circles.

Turning her back to the crowd, Nena slowed her body movements as the salsa music morphed into a sultry tune that conjured visions of a smoky cantina and frantic, sweaty table sex. She hooked her fingers in the waistband of her panties and dragged them down her lush, thick ass. Heat surged through his belly as inch by delicious inch of her silky skin was revealed. A glittering rhinestone thong clung to her body. Panties around her ankles, she slowly bent forward at the waist and shook the plump flesh to the delight of her fans.

With a loud smack on her bottom, Nena straightened and stepped out of her panties. Those too she flung into the audience. Yet another scuffle broke out among the men but Zel was oblivious. He couldn't take his eyes off the gyrating goddess before him. Tongue against her teeth, she undulated like a belly dancer, one hand buried in her hair, the other brushing against her stomach. A tiny triangle of sequined fabric barely covered the vee at the top of her thighs. He desperately prayed it would soon be removed.

Zel's eyes widened as she picked up a bottle of lotion from the short stand next to the tub. Across the pulsing throng of patrons, their eyes locked. Rather naughtily, she ran her fingers down the length of the pearly tube. With a salacious smile, she flicked her pointed tongue across the top. His cock throbbed as if she had just licked the head. Rubbing the tube between her luscious breasts, she popped the lid and squeezed the bottle so hard, white lotion shot all over her breasts. The symbolism wasn't lost on clamoring crowd.

Wearing that dreamy, sexy expression, Nena looked like a woman thoroughly debauched. She carelessly dropped the bottle and rubbed the creamy lotion down her gently curved belly. Ever so cautiously, she climbed into the bathtub. Armed with a dripping sponge, she dribbled water down her front before lathering the lotion covering her skin. As it foamed, Zel realized it was body wash.

Quite indecently, Nena soaped her body. Zel imagined his hands roaming her slick skin, his fingers kneading those large breasts and slipping beneath that oh so tiny swatch of cloth covering her pussy.

All too soon, Nena lowered herself into the tub. Just as the music began to fade, she placed her toes against the rim of the tub and grasped the sides, arching her back as she lifted out of the bath, soapy water dripping from her glistening, gorgeous body. It was truly a sight to behold.

And then the lights were snuffed and the curtain fell. Pandemonium ensued. Zel couldn't whistle or hoot or clap. Rendered breathless, he knew there was only one thing to be done.

He had to meet her.

CHAPTER TWO

S AFE INSIDE HER dressing room, Sara Contreras dropped the now damp robe her sister had thrust upon her as she left the stage. She unfurled one of the folded towels resting on her dressing table. As she pressed the towel to her neck, her legs trembled and belly quivered. Curious, she slipped a hand between her thighs, tucking the fingers under the rhinestone thong. Her clit throbbed beneath her fingertips, and she inhaled a shaky breath as she realized how aroused she was.

In all the years she had performed on stage as Nena Rubens, never once had she been aroused by a patron. As a general rule, she offered the body shot to whomever had paid for the performance, but the second she had clapped eyes on the blond Adonis in the front row, she'd decided to switch things up a bit. For the first time in a long time she'd been able to separate one face from the crowd. She had danced as if doing a private show. Judging by the crowd's reaction, they had loved it.

Fanning her face, Sara grabbed a bottle of water and swallowed an icy sip. *You have to calm down!* She couldn't walk into her autograph and schmoozing session all hot and bothered. It wouldn't be professional.

Loud rapping at the door grabbed her attention. Expecting

Lucy, her sister-slash-assistant, on the other side, she grabbed her robe and slipped into it before wrenching open the door. She recoiled in surprise. Instead of being eye to eye with a spunky brunette, Sara suddenly had an eyeful of one of the very last men on earth she ever wanted to see again. She reacted on instinct and slammed the door in Ramsay Ramirez's face.

But Ramsay was too fast. He had *always* been too fast. He gripped the door and shoved it forward, causing Sara to stumble back toward the vanity. She quickly grabbed the slipper chair and held it up like a shield. Eyeing her abusive stepbrother, she warned, "I'll scream if you take another step closer."

He grinned evilly. "I'll take my chances."

Certain he meant that, she shakily insisted, "You're not allowed to be here. The restraining order says—"

"That judge was in Texas. We're standing in Nevada right now, Sarita."

Feeling sick at the sound of her nickname coming from his mouth, she shook her head. "The restraining order follows me across state lines. You are not allowed to be here."

"So scream," Ramsay said with a tired shrug. "Ten bucks says I can haul your fat ass out of here before anyone comes running."

Cold dread gripped her stomach. He would do it, too. He *had* done worse.

"Is there a problem here?"

Her panicked gaze jumped to the doorway where the handsome blond fighter now stood. His stance was one of practiced aggression, his feet spaced evenly apart, his weight shifted back and his hands relaxed but ready to strike. He towered over Ramsay by two or three inches and had a leaner, meaner build.

Relieved to have a champion so close at hand, she shot the fighter a desperate glance. *Please,* she begged silently, *make him leave me alone.*

"Who the fuck are you?" Ramsay asked in that incredibly aggressive way of his.

The fighter didn't even blink. He seemed wholly unfazed by Ramsay's asshole routine or the Hermanos gang tattoos on her stepbrother's neck and arms. "I'm her date," the blond lied. "Who the fuck are *you*?"

"Her brother," Ramsay ground out between clenched teeth.

"Stepbrother," Sara quickly inserted. "He's my *stepbrother*, and there is a permanent restraining order in place. He's not allowed to be here."

"Then it's time for you to leave," the fighter said. Stepping forward, he grabbed Ramsay by the back of the neck and grasped his wrist, wrenching it behind his back and forcing her ex into a painful bend that caused him to yowl. He marched Ramsay out of the dressing room and down the hall, disappearing from her view. There was quite a commotion a short time later. Sara held her breath as she listened to the men arguing. Something big and heavy slammed into a wall. Ramsay? The fighter?

Dropping the chair, she rushed to the door and hid behind it. She pushed it mostly closed, just in case Ramsay got free. He was going to be thoroughly pissed off after this, and if he managed to make his way backstage again, it probably wasn't going to end well for her.

Heavy footsteps echoed in the hall. She cowered behind the door and held her breath. The footsteps stopped outside the door. A wave of panic engulfed her.

"Ma'am?" Three swift knocks on the partially closed door followed. "He's gone."

She stepped to the side and peered out the crack between the door and the frame. At first, all she could see was a white poplin shirt and classic black blazer. She tilted her head back and breathed out a sigh of relief upon seeing the fighter again.

My rescuer.

"Thank you." Sara opened the door to let him inside. A moment too late, she remembered she was almost naked and only wearing a robe, but it wasn't as if he hadn't already seen everything already while she danced. Still, she felt vulnerable and exposed in a way that was almost too intimate.

His icy blue eyes raked down her body. She seized the opportunity to size him up as well. With those broad shoulders and that angular jaw, he possessed the fierce look of a warrior. Even now, completely relaxed, he stood like a fighter. Somehow he managed to look powerful and capable without the aggressiveness she had seen earlier. He made her feel secure and safe.

She imagined the rippled muscles hidden beneath his shirt and mustered tremendous control to keep her greedy fingers still. He was so close she could smell the subtle cedar notes of his cologne. She inhaled discreetly and buzzed on his manly scent.

"I'm sorry." He stepped back from the doorway, obviously discomfited by her half-naked state. His accent—almost

Russian but not quite—piqued her interest. "Should I come back later?"

"No!" Embarrassed by her hasty response, she added, "I mean, I'd like you to stay. I'd like to explain that mess you just witnessed."

"You don't owe me any explanations. I was happy to help." His expression turned dark. "That guy is an asshole. If you have a restraining order, you need to talk to the club security, to your hotel security and to the local police. He needs to be trespassed and run out of this town."

"He's not so easily dissuaded," she replied quietly. She didn't think this stranger wanted to hear about the very estranged husband she had back in Houston or her ties to an Albanian loan shark who had given her a start dancing in his first club. "There is a lot of ugly history there."

The knight who had just saved her raised an eyebrow. "I see."

"Yeah," she laughed nervously. Drawing together the lapels of her robe, she pulled them tight and tied the sash at her waist. "Please come inside."

With a nod, he accepted her invitation and entered the dressing room. She closed the door behind him. Thinking of the little white lie he had told, she teased, "So...what's your name? I should know your name if you're my date, right?"

"I shouldn't have lied like that, but I wasn't sure what else to do." He smiled and extended his hand. "Zel Tesla."

"Sara Contreras." She clasped his warm, rough hand. Noticing the confusion wrinkling his forehead, she quickly explained, "Nena is just a stage name." Certain he was one of the fighters in town for the big match, she asked, "Is Zel your real name or just a fighting name?"

"I fight under my real name. Most of us do." He hesitated. "Do you watch MMA fights?"

"Not really," she admitted. "I'm not a big fan of violence."

"Oh. Right." Was he thinking of Ramsay? Putting the pieces together?

Hoping she hadn't hurt his feelings, she hastily added, "But, um, I'm interested in these fights because you're my hometown boys."

"You're from Houston?"

She nodded. "Born and raised. I couldn't pass up the chance to book a gig the same weekend when the men from Ivan's warehouse are fighting."

"You know Ivan Markovic?" He seemed surprised by the connection.

"We aren't close or anything, but we have a few friends in common. I actually saw him fight way back in the day when he used to brawl in those cages at the old meatpacking plant," she admitted.

"But you said you don't like fights," he pointed out.

"I don't. I didn't." She swallowed anxiously as memories she had long since buried tried to resurface. "I was involved with a man who liked them. He was trying to climb the underworld ladder and those fights were the place to be seen." Allowing herself a moment to reminisce, she said, "I still remember the day the Red Army landed in Houston and started their invasion. It was chaos. The old players—the motorcycle gangs and the Mexican street gangs and the Vietnamese crews—weren't ready for the kind of war that Nikolai brought."

Zel seemed taken aback. He fidgeted with his left hand as he said, "You seem to know a lot about the underworld."

Her gaze settled on the barely visible peek of a familiar tattoo marking the spot between Zel's left thumb and forefinger. Realizing they had more in common than just Ivan, she swiped her right thumb over the same spot on her left hand and cleaned away the makeup covering her mark. Lifting her hand, she said, "So do you."

Zel's smiling expression collapsed as he glimpsed the tiny tattoo on her skin that marked her as a person in the Albanian mafia's debt. "I guess I don't have to ask if you know Besian."

"I know him. Probably better than you," she allowed. "But my debt is paid. Yours?"

He shook his head. "Soon."

"The fight?" she guessed.

"Yes." Hesitantly, he asked, "Were you one of Besian's girls?"

"Would it matter if I was?" She had never been embarrassed or made a secret of her humble beginnings on a badly lit Houston strip club stage.

"No," he answered quickly. "I don't care about those kinds of things. We're all just trying to make a living and survive. I was only curious about how you ended up in his debt."

"That's a long story."

"I'd like to hear it. Tonight," he added with a smoldering glance.

The offer hung in the air as a promise of night she wouldn't ever forget. Wondering if she was reading him right, she said, "Maybe."

"While you decide if you're going to tell me that story," he presented her with the program from that night's show, "would you mind signing this for me?"

"I don't mind." She crossed to her dressing table and chose a marker from the cup Lucy had left. Glancing at the mirror mounted over the table, Sara noticed Zel's eyes trained on the outline of her ass through the clinging robe. Her tummy fluttered as she realized he hadn't just come for an autograph. If that was all he'd wanted, he could have waited for the meet and greet.

No, he'd come for something else.

Something she was more than willing to give, especially after the way he had come to her aid. If nothing else, he had earned a proper thank-you kiss. Before Ramsay had appeared without warning or invite, she had been fantasizing about this very man. Refusing to let her ex-con stepbrother take anything else away from her, even this fleeting moment of possible happiness, she pushed that horrid encounter out of her mind and focused only the man standing before her now.

With a seductive swing of her hips, Sara approached Zel and took the program from his hand, making sure to graze her fingertips against his skin. She smiled coquettishly and placed the program against his chest. The tip of the marker raced across the bottom of her vixenish pose.

Her signature in place, she toyed with a button on his shirt. His heartbeat sprinted beneath her fingertips and she took that as her cue to continue. Rising on tiptoes, Sara languidly sniffed his neck and lazily purred, "You smell amazing."

Tiny goose bumps erupted along his neck. The corners of her lips curved with a smug grin. "Do you want to kiss me?"

"Are you serious?" The vein in his throat jumped. He seemed taken aback by her rather brazen behavior, but also very, very interested.

"Yes." She smiled saucily and pressed her plump lips to his. He stiffened in surprise but quickly relaxed as she sucked his lower lip between hers. Anxious quivers rocked her belly. A hungry groan escaped his throat and vibrated through her lips. His strong arms wound around her back, and he hauled her against his chest. Fingers sifting through his short hair, Sara captured his mouth in a sensuous kiss. Her tongue slipped between his lips, searching for his.

What are you doing? You don't know this man. Slow down.

But she didn't want to slow down. Kissing this man felt incredible. She couldn't remember the last time she had felt so alive. She trembled inside, her heart racing and her breaths coming faster and faster.

As their tongues mated, Zel's hands rode the curve of her back and grasped her bottom through the flimsy fabric of her robe. Her eyes widened as his cock stabbed her soft belly. The length of his hardness made her curious so she slid her hand down his abs and over his belt buckle.

When she grasped him through his trousers, Zel groaned and pumped his hips. Throwing caution to the wind, she pushed him backward until his back hit the door. They traded frantic kisses as Zel dragged her robe down around her shoulders. Sara let her arms drop and, with a little shake, sent the robe fluttering around her ankles.

Standing in just her rhinestone thong and tassels, she felt incredibly sexy and just a little bit vulnerable. Zel groped her bare cheeks with his big hands. He peppered her jaw and neck with kisses. Hands on her shoulders, he spun her around and pulled her ass against his cock. His rough palms caressed her breasts and belly.

When he tugged on her nipple tassels, she sucked in a sharp breath. He nibbled her neck and sucked on the curve of her throat. Eyes closed, she pushed back against his cock, wiggling her ass to tease him.

As his fingers found their way to her slick cleft, her eyes flew open and caught their reflection in the mirror. Her heart raced as she watched his hand beneath the thin triangle of fabric covering her sex. Zel's gaze burned hers in the mirror across the room.

When a thick finger slid inside her pussy, Sara whimpered and bucked. His thumb settled over her clit and flicked the swollen nub. Zel's dexterity amazed her as he worked her pussy in a way she had never experienced. Her knees trembled as he fingered her slick sheath and rubbed her clit with just the right amount of speed and pressure. His teeth grazed her shoulder as he alternated suckling the sensitive spot with teasing nibbles. Sara's toes curled at the sensual assault. Her breath hitched as she approached orgasm.

"I want to see you come." Zel's whisper tickled her ear. "Look at me."

Sara couldn't deny his request. Their eyes locked in the mirror. For the briefest of moments, she wondered how the hell this was happening. Twenty minutes ago, she was fantasizing about touching him. Now he was doing these wicked, wicked things to her body.

As the waves of ecstasy crashed down upon her, she pressed her pussy into his hand, milking his digits for every last ounce of sensation. Only his arm curled around her waist kept her from falling to the floor in a boneless, quivering heap. She shivered when he gently removed his fingers from her G-string. He brought the shiny fingers to his lips and sucked them clean. The sight drove her wild.

Suddenly Sara was overwhelmed with the need to taste him. She turned around and dropped to her knees. Her greedy fingers tugged on his belt buckle and unzipped his fly. She grabbed a handful of his shirt and pulled it free from his trousers. Her nose nuzzled his bellybutton and happy trail. Teeth grasping the waistband of his black boxer briefs, she started to drag them down.

And then there was a knock at the door.

"Sara?" Lucy's voice penetrated the wood. "Are you okay? They security guys just told me there was some kind of altercation!"

Cursing her sister's timing, Sara cleared her throat of its huskiness before replying, "I'll explain everything in a few minutes. I need to finish getting dressed."

"You're sure you're okay?"

"I'm fine."

"Well it's only ten minutes until the meet 'n' greet. You need any help?"

"No."

"All right. I'll be back in a sec to escort you."

"Okay." As Lucy left, Sara rested her forehead against Zel's rock-hard stomach. She could actually feel the ridges of his muscular abs and wanted nothing more than to get him naked so she could see and taste and touch all of him. "I'm sorry."

He cupped her chin and tipped it gently. His warm smile

reassured her. "It's okay. I understand."

"Are you sure?" Some part of her expected Zel to get salty about not getting his way.

"I'm sure." Like a gentleman, he helped her stand. He bent down, snatched her robe from the floor and draped it around her bare shoulders. Leaning in, he kissed the side of her neck. "What we just did was beyond my wildest expectations. I was really just hoping you'd let me buy you a drink."

Meeting his heated gaze, she smiled. "I'd let you buy me a drink."

"I'd like to see you again." He traced her collarbone with his finger. "Maybe we can have dinner?"

His hopeful tone made her practically giddy. "Tonight?"

He nodded.

Sara scurried to her purse on the corner chair and rifled through the contents. She found the spare key to her penthouse suite and raced back to him. "You'll need this to access the elevator to my floor. I'll be back in my room by eleven."

Zel pocketed the key. "I'll be there."

She trembled with the promise of a night she'd never forget. "So I'll see you then?"

He leaned down and kissed her hungrily. "Count on it."

Flashing that ever so sexy grin, Zel opened the door and slipped into the hallway. Sara collapsed against the door, barely able to breathe. *What did I just do?*

Fear and anxiety drenched her in a cold wave as she thought of Ramsay. That burst of intense pleasure she had shared with Zel seemed like something out of a dream world when she remembered the menacing look on her stepbrother's face.

If he had come all this way to harass and intimidate her, he was never going to stop. Not for the first time, she wondered if picking up and moving overseas really was the best option for dealing with him.

Wanting to escape from the ugly reality awaiting her, she decided to push Ramsay out of her mind. She finished changing into the dress she had chosen tonight, a fun little rockabilly style number to fit with her usual fifties pin-up style, and fixed her hair and makeup. Lucy returned while she was primping and helped her into a pair of candy apple red heels and pearl jewelry.

"So?" Lucy asked.

"So what?"

"The altercation?"

She didn't want to upset her sister, but this wasn't a secret she could keep. "It was Ramsay."

Lucy's face turned pale. "He's here? In Vegas? How? When did he get out of the pen?"

Sara shrugged. "I don't know. We didn't have a chance to talk."

"What are we going to do?" Lucy asked carefully, her face a mask of concern and worry.

"I'll talk to security and the police when we're done with the meet-and-greet."

"What do you think he wants?" Lucy stuffed a few necessities in a clutch and handed it over.

Sara studied her reflection in the mirror. "What he always wants—money."

"Fuck that guy," Lucy said angrily. "Just fuck him so hard."

Sara smiled sadly at her sister. "We can't let him twist us up like this. It's exactly what he wants. He thrives on manipulating people and gets off on upsetting us. We have to just let it go."

"He's dangerous. You can't just let it go."

"I know he's dangerous," Sara murmured quietly. She had the healed fractures and nose reconstruction bills to prove it. "But I won't let him rule my life anymore."

Lucy embraced her in a side-hug. "We'll figure it out, okay? I don't want you to worry."

"I'm not worried," she lied. Perking up, she embraced her inner vixen and motioned toward the door. "We should go. I have plans for later."

"With that fighter I saw sneaking out of here a few minutes ago?" Lucy eyed her with a mischievous smile.

Sara blushed. "Maybe."

"He's a nice guy. If the press about him is to be believed," she added.

"Oh?" Lucy and her wife were diehard fans of mixed-martial arts and boxing. They spent more on pay-per-view matches than Sara did on shoes. If anyone had the inside info on Zel, it would be Lucy.

"He has this whole tragic story. He was an orphanage kid. Then he was in the military in Croatia. Eventually he came to the US—to Houston, actually—with his baby boy. That was, like, seven or eight year ago. He's had a really successful career. Lots of really spectacular wins. He always finishes strong."

"A son?" Sara seized on that bit of information. "He's not married, right?"

"No." Lucy bopped her shoulder. "But *you* are."

"I'm separated," she insisted hotly. "For nearly ten years! I'd be long divorced if Lalo would just stop the bullshit and sign the papers."

"He can't control you if he signs the papers."

Lucy was right, of course. After Luscious Lingerie, the plus-size clothing company Sara owned, had started to churn major bucks, she had offered her estranged husband a sizeable payday to let her go free, but he'd refused. Actually, he had countered with a higher number and the demand that she let him have her for one more weekend. Knowing what kind of damage he could do in forty-eight hours, Sara had ended the negotiations and continued living her life as a single but not really single woman.

"Zel was a single father," Lucy said.

"Was?" That didn't sound good at all.

"His son died about a year ago? Maybe fourteen or fifteen months ago?"

Sara no longer had to wonder about that sadness in his pale eyes. It was the haunted look of a man who had lost something important and impossible to replace. "Oh my God! How awful!"

"He was a just a kid. Maybe six years old? I don't remember all the details. I just remember that he stepped away from the ring for about two years, right around the time his son became really sick. He's been fighting again, taking small matches and doing well. This is his first big match since stepping back in the ring. They're saying it might be his last."

Sara tried to wrap her head around all of that information. She hardly knew the man, but she ached for his loss. How terrible to lose a child! From what little Lucy had said, it sounded as if Zel's son had been sick. To go through all of that fear and stress and grief alone? It must have been incredibly hard on him.

As she followed Lucy out of the dressing room and down to the meet-and-greet, Sara decided that she and Zel both could use a little escape tonight. Vegas had their motto for a reason. Tonight, they were the perfect couple to indulge in a little one-night-stand therapy.

Because if anyone needs a torrid escape from reality, it's us…

CHAPTER THREE

A MPED UP FOR his secret date with Sara, Zel paced his hotel room. He glanced at his watch for the hundredth time and decided it was time to go. He tried to ignore the quiver of guilt irritating his stomach. There were strict gym rules for all the fighters on Ivan's roster and those included staying away from women before fights. It was an old school thing, but Ivan's rules were his rules. They weren't meant to be broken.

He'll never know. Zel was certain he could sneak out and back into his room without his coach ever knowing that he had left. The thought of lying to Ivan after all their years as friends wasn't one he liked, but Zel couldn't ignore the pull he felt toward Sara.

After so many months of self-imposed celibacy, she had awakened something dark and powerful in him. He needed to see her again. He needed to taste her again. He wanted to know what it was like to be inside her.

"Where are you going?"

Zel had barely closed the door to his hotel room when Ivan's gruff voice registered. *Well. Fuck.*

He glanced over his shoulder and spotted his hulking Russian coach holding a bottle of champagne in one hand and a silver ice bucket in the other. He'd lost his suit jacket and tie.

His shirt was unbuttoned at the neck low enough to reveal the tips of the onion dome cathedral tattooed on his chest. His sleeves were rolled up to his elbows and his pants were wrinkled. For a man who was always so neatly put together, Ivan's appearance spoke volumes.

"Where are you going?" Zel shot back.

"Room service was taking forever, and I needed champagne and ice." Ivan fixed his discerning stare on him. "Where are you going?"

"Just headed out," Zel said, deliberately evading the question.

"For?" Ivan narrowed his eyes. "You know they have room service or concierge if you need something."

"What I need will probably get me arrested if I try to order it through the concierge," Zel admitted, trying to make light of the situation.

"You're going to see that dancer aren't you?" Ivan never missed a beat. Many people stupider than Zel had made the mistake of underestimating him. Somehow Ivan always managed to see or hear about any indiscretions. Before Zel could decide whether to deny or admit to that charge, Ivan shook his head. "I was told that you went backstage for an autograph. I knew it was total bullshit."

"It's not like that, Vanya."

"And that fight I heard about? Huh? The security guards who went running backstage?" Ivan dared him to lie. "I suppose you didn't have anything to do with that?"

"It wasn't a real fight. I just tossed some guy out the back door."

"Some guy? What guy?"

Zel rubbed the back of his neck and grimaced. "She was being harassed."

"By?"

"Her stepbrother."

Ivan swore in Russian. "You stay the fuck away from Ramsay Ramirez, Zel. He's a violent pig who can't be trusted."

Ivan's reaction to the mention of her stepbrother confirmed what she had told him. "Sara said she was from Houston and that she knew you."

"Oh, I remember Sara Contreras," Ivan assured him. "And what I remember is dangerous." Shaking his head, Ivan changed his grip on the champagne bottle and jabbed a warning finger in Zel's direction. "Stay away from her. At least until the fight is over, Zel. The last fucking thing you need is pussy drama."

Ivan was right. He was always right when it came to things like this. But Zel couldn't stay away from her.

"It is the last thing I need," Zel agreed, "but I'm still going to see her."

Disappointment radiated from Ivan in unbearable waves. "If you want to fuck around and get your head all mixed up with some dancer, that's your business. It's your life."

Shaking his head, Ivan pivoted away from Zel. He took a few steps before calling back, "Remember what's on the line, Zel. Remember why you fight."

Anger surged through him at Ivan's patronizing tone. "Do you think I've forgotten? Huh? Do you have any idea what it's like to wake up every morning knowing that I'm not going to see my son's face? That I'm not going to hear him laugh? That I'm not going to read him a bedtime story or hug him good-night?"

Ivan stopped and turned slowly. The guilt on etched into his coach's face was an expression Zel had never seen from him. Apologetic, Ivan walked back until they were only a few feet apart. "I had no right to say that to you."

Zel expelled a rough breath. "Maybe not but you're right to question what I'm thinking," he allowed. "You're my coach. It's your job to look out for me."

Ivan tucked the champagne bottle under his other arm and clamped his massive hand on Zel's shoulder. Giving it a squeeze, he said, "I know how hard you've worked to come back after losing Matthias. You've put in so many hours to get back into prime fighting shape. I don't want to see all that sweat and sacrifice go to waste."

"It won't."

Ivan studied his face as if seeking answers. "You've been through so much, Zel. You've lost more than I can comprehend." He hesitated. "Maybe you need to blow off some steam." Ivan lowered his hand from Zel's shoulder. "That's what Vegas is all about, right?"

Zel reacted with surprise at his coach's suggestion that he go out tonight and have a good time. "Are you sure?"

"You're going anyway." Ivan shrugged. "I may as well give you my approval so you aren't sneaking around and getting into trouble behind my back."

Before Zel could answer, Erin appeared behind Ivan, poking her head around the corner of the hotel hallway. "Evie?"

Zel's mouth twitched as he suppressed a smile at Erin's little pet name for her husband. Ivan glanced back at his wife and frowned when she stepped around the corner in a flimsy black robe that barely skimmed the middle of her thighs. Judging by the way she was holding the robe together in the front, she wasn't wearing much underneath it. Even from his distance, Zel could see the prominent love bite on her neck and the bright red imprints of Ivan's fingertips on her thighs. He didn't have to think very hard to fill in those blanks.

"You were gone a long time," she said, lingering there. "I was worried."

Ivan's expression softened. "I ran into Zel. I didn't mean to worry you."

"Well quit harassing him and get back in our suite!" Erin crooked her finger in a come-hither motion. "Or else I'll have to find someone else to come play with me."

There was no mistaking the lusty gleam in Ivan's eyes that her teasing inspired. He glanced back at Zel and lowered his voice, "You're a good fighter, Zel. You've earned this chance to fight for big money. I know what it will mean if you win."

Ivan didn't have to say the words *loan shark* for Zel to understand. It was an open secret around the gym that Zel still owed a hefty balance to the Beciraj crime family that had financed his escape from Croatia with his young, sick son. He had fought underground in the bloody prize tournaments for the family to pay off his first debt—but then Matthias's heart had grown weaker and a transplant was necessary.

Without insurance, he'd had no choice but to go back to Besian Beciraj, hat in hand, and ask for another even larger loan. By then, he had been fighting professionally, but the money hadn't been very good yet. Each month, he fell farther and farther behind because of interest. And then, when Matthias's condition had worsened, he had put his payments—and his career—on hold to focus on keeping his son alive while they waited for a transplant.

But after the failed transplant, Zel hadn't cared at all whether the knee breakers came after him. In some ways, he would have welcomed the physical pain that would have accompanied a collector's beat-down, but they never came. Besian had shown a surprising amount of flexibility and generosity. He hadn't once sent Jet or Devil or Ben around to collect the late and even later payments. He had simply waited for Zel to come to him and promise to make good on his debt. It had taken more than a year for Zel to work through the depression and grief, to find a way to keep living and moving forward with his life without his son.

There was a lot of money riding on this fight. Zel wasn't expected to win, but if he did—and he planned to do just that—he would finally escape his debt. Besian had been very clear that the family had placed a number of large bets. If he won the bout, Zel would be free.

Broke as hell, he thought with some frustration, *but free.*

"You said you wanted to retire on top," Ivan reminded him. "You wanted to end your career on your terms. If you still want that, you have to keep your head straight. Go have fun with this dancer tonight—and then be in the gym tomorrow morning ready to train."

His counsel given, Ivan ate up the distance to his smiling wife with long, determined strides. He murmured something to Erin that Zel couldn't hear. Whatever it was, it must have been dirty because Erin blushed bright red and then spun on her heel and dashed back toward their room. Zel heard her squeal with laughter. A moment later, the telltale smack of

Ivan's hand whacking her bottom echoed in the hallway. Erin yelped. Ivan's dark laughter faded away as a door was closed.

Not for the first time, Zel envied Ivan's relationship with his wife. Lately, Erin had been spending a lot of time at the gym, taking over the day-to-day operations for her husband. After watching the couple interact on a daily basis, it was clear how very much Erin loved her husband, and Ivan utterly adored and worshipped her. The little touches, the smiles, the laughter—Zel craved that closeness and intimacy.

It had taken him months and months to get to the point where he no longer experienced extreme guilt when he thought of his future, of the life that he would live without Matthias. Tonight he felt almost optimistic. There was no telling whether this date he had planned with Sara would go anywhere. Maybe it would end as a simple one-night stand or maybe it would lead to something new and interesting. Either way, Ivan was right. He *did* need to blow off some steam.

But what did Ivan know about Sara's history that had his coach so twisted? There had to be a story there, probably a story that included some serious underworld drama.

His mind went wild with possibilities as he walked to the nearest elevator and waited for the next car. He went straight down to the lobby and crossed to the private bank of elevators for accessing the exclusive areas of the hotel. Showing the hotel keycard wasn't enough for the security guard, but a quick call to the penthouse and the guard confirmed he was expected upstairs.

Zel wondered if this extra level of security was in place because of Sara's run-in with her stepbrother. He had a bad feeling about that guy. His years living on the edge of the criminal underworld had taught him how to spot an asshole like that at fifty paces. That guy wasn't going to leave her alone unless someone made him. He was the type of monster who got off on playing power games. Maybe it was time someone played head games with him...

Pushing all thoughts of the stepbrother from his mind, Zel replayed their wild kiss in the dressing room. His limbs trembled as he stepped off the elevator and into a private hallway. There was only one door straight ahead. As he strode toward it, his dick leapt in his pants. He was so hard it hurt. Just the thought of burying his face in Sara's sweet pussy threatened to make him come in his pants. He couldn't ever remember being so turned-on in his life.

His mind reeled from the surreal turn his visit to her dressing room had taken. At best, Zel had been hoping to snag a dinner date. Holding Sara close as he worked her into a frenzied state with his fingers had never even crossed his mind. Her delicious taste still lingered on his lips.

Clenching his shaking fingers, Zel rapped his knuckles against the door. He expected to wait but the door swung inward almost immediately. His eyes widened at the sight of Sara, naked and freshly showered, her damp hair curling around her shoulders. He raked his hungry gaze over those full breasts and the gentle curve of her belly. Desperate to get his hands on her plump flesh, Zel lifted his hand and let a strip of condoms unfold for her approval.

In a flash, Sara snatched a handful of his shirt and dragged him inside the penthouse. He kicked the door shut behind him and trailed her like a puppy through the various rooms of the upscale suite. His eyes trained on the hypnotic swing of her wide hips and the jiggle of her voluptuous ass. Naughty visions filtered through his mind.

When they reached the bedroom, Sara pounced on him. Her fingers made quick work of divesting his clothing. Dropping the condoms, Zel helped speed up the process, kicking off his shoes and tearing off his shirt. He'd barely peeled off his boxer briefs before Sara shoved him onto the bed. He fell back against the fluffy comforter, his feet still flat on the floor. In an instant, her hot, wet mouth was wrapped around the head of his cock. The sensation of her velvety tongue flicking at the underside of his dick knocked the breath from his lungs. Her slick lips enveloped his shaft and slid down the length.

Eyes closed, Zel enjoyed the unbelievable feeling of her tongue and lips lavishing attention on his cock. Her hands joined the party, one stroking his shaft, the other playing with his balls. His hips pumped subtly in reaction to the delicious stimulation. When Zel lifted his head and watched his cock disappear down her throat, he nearly shot off.

Not ready to lose it just yet, he gently pulled away from her mouth. She cast a confused look his way. "Did I do something wrong?"

He shook his head. "You did everything right. I want to come with you—later."

Mischief sparkled in Sara's brown eyes. "Later?"

"Right now I want you to get up on this bed and put your ass in the air." Zel grinned at the enthusiastic expression on Sara's face. She hastily complied. He slid off the bed and knelt behind her. Wasting no time, Zel palmed her plump cheeks and dived into her pussy. Sara squealed with delight as he lapped at her core. He nibbled at her dusky lips and traced them toward her pulsing clit.

As he suckled the nub, Zel slipped a pair of fingers into her. Sara moaned and pushed back against his thrusting fingers. The clenching feeling around his fingers transmitted straight to his dick and made him mad with desire. To keep his mind off his throbbing cock, Zel concentrated on her clit, tugging the bud between his lips and flicking his tongue against it.

Howling into the comforter, Sara clenched her thighs together and abruptly broke contact. "You're going to kill me," she panted.

Smirking, Zel wiped his mouth on the back of his hand. He stretched to reach the discarded strip of condoms and tore one loose. With a rip of his teeth, he opened the package and hastily applied the latex sheath. He climbed onto the bed where Sara knelt, facing him. Reclining against the pile of pillows, Zel motioned to his cock. "Ride me?"

Sara's eyes lit up and she nodded happily. Looking incredibly sexy, she crawled toward him and straddled his hips. She grasped the base of his thick cock and lifted her ass, lining up their bodies for the ultimate joining. Satisfied moans escaped their lips as she took ever last inch of his shaft. She sat still for a moment, as if savoring the new sensation of being filled by him.

His hands moved to her thick waist, his fingers grasping her plump hips as he guided her slow movements. She swayed back and forth and swiveled her hips in circles. The look on her face told him all he needed to know. She was loving every minute of riding his cock.

Bit-by-bit Sara's pace quickened, as did the force of her strokes. Hands on his chest, she shifted her weight from her knees to her feet and bounced hard on him. He was taken aback by the vision of this luscious beauty. Those gorgeous tits bounced just inches from his face, tempting him with their rosy peaks. Licking his lips, he leaned forward and sucked a stiff nipple into his mouth. Sara whimpered and pushed against him. A smile played upon her pouting lips.

"What?" Zel's curiosity got the best of him.

Sara didn't bother stopping her wild ride. Grinning playfully, she replied, "You're the first man I'm not afraid of breaking."

He laughed and snapped his hips a few times, meeting her downward strokes. Lips returning to her breasts, he wrapped his arms around her and embraced her as she gyrated atop him. She cupped the back of his neck and made the most primal noises he'd ever heard.

When she slowed her pace, he glanced up questioningly. Breathless, she kissed him. "Now I want to come with you."

His stomach flip-flopped. "On your back."

Sara lifted off and fell back onto the comforter, her head pointed toward the foot of the bed. Black waves fanned around her head and framed her beautiful face. He planted kisses on her knee, up along her thigh and across her belly as he moved over her. A soft sigh escaped her lips as Zel slid into place, his cock finding its home again. His fingers tangled in her hair as he thrust languidly and made love to her mouth. Her hands roamed his back, fingernails trailing up and down his skin.

When Sara's hands gripped his backside, Zel understood the message. He deepened his thrusts and moved faster, taking her with sharp strokes. Sara rose up beneath him, meeting each pump of his hips. As they raced toward their shared release, the fervency of their mating took on an animalistic tone. Grunting and groaning, they kissed frantically and groped at one another. The bed shook with their exertions.

At the sound of her changing breaths, Zel knew she was close. He finally released the grip he'd had on his own orgasm and let the trembling sensation build at the base of his spine. Her fingers tightened on his biceps just seconds before she threw back her head and cried out. She undulated beneath him, her pussy rhythmically clasping and releasing his cock. His final thrusts were so deep and hard he nearly fucked her off the edge of the bed. With a growl, he came, spilling his cum into the latex reservoir.

When he shifted his weight, they tumbled off the bed and landed in a tangled heap on the floor. Sara let out a surprised *oof* before giggling. Smiling, he tried to kick off the comforter and top sheet wound around his ankle. Realizing it was a lost cause, he rolled onto his back and hauled Sara against him. Her infectious laughter took hold of him.

Cuddled together, they shook with amusement before settling down. Her fingers drew lazy shapes on his abs. He caressed her silky shoulder as he allowed his mind to wander. Only Sara's growling stomach could penetrate his thoughts. Amused, he glanced down at her. She smiled apologetically and shrugged. "Room service?"

CHAPTER FOUR

CURLED UP IN the corner of the cushy couch, Sara noshed on a rather tasty cheeseburger and sweet potato fries. Some women would have felt self-conscious chowing down in front of the man who'd very nearly fucked them senseless, but not Sara. She was hungry so she was eating. End of story.

Zel sipped his green tea. He had picked at a light meal of salad and chicken, his food choices deliberately low in calories but high in protein. "Your suite is much nicer than mine."

"I danced at the owner's sixtieth birthday party a few months ago. Sweet guy, really lovely wife," she added, remembering the warm couple. "Are you staying here too?"

He nodded and set aside his teacup. "The hotel is sponsoring part of the fight. We've got a floor to ourselves."

"Nifty." She swiped a fry through ketchup and eyed Zel curiously. "You don't strike me as the cage-fighting type."

Bemusement colored his features. "And what does a cage fighter look like?"

She shrugged. "Generally cage fighters are the guys who don't seem to have many other options. You're obviously very intelligent. You could have done anything with your life, I think. You're not very brutish so I don't get the feeling that you fight because you love violence and blood and pain. You don't seem to have a criminal past or be tied in with one of the syndicates so…?"

There was a far-off look in his eyes before he finally replied. "Sometimes we find ourselves doing things we never imagined for the people we love."

"For your son?" she asked carefully.

Zel's gaze snapped to her face. He narrowed his eyes. "Yes. Who told you?"

"My sister follows the fight leagues. She mentioned that you had lost your son recently." Touching his hand, she said, "I'm so sorry, Zel. That must have been very difficult."

"Thank you," he answered quietly. With a sad smile, he said, "Matthias was such a sweet boy. He always had a smile on his face, even at the end when the pain was terrible and he could hardly breathe."

"Was he sick?" she asked softly.

"He was born with a very serious heart defect. Hypoplastic Left Heart," Zel named the condition. "Basically, his heart was only half developed. After he was born, they were able to keep him alive long enough to get him to a proper hospital in Greece where he had three procedures. The surgeries would help him live for a while, but he needed a heart transplant. Houston is one of the best places in the world for babies with heart problems. I knew that if I could get him to Houston he would have a fighting chance."

"So you borrowed money from Besian?"

"Luka," Zel corrected. "One of my family members worked for him. They put us in touch, and he offered me money if I would go to Houston and work for Besian. I couldn't say no. I had to do whatever was necessary for my son's life."

"Of course," she agreed. "I would have done the same thing."

"Once I got to Houston, I did some enforcing and collections. They realized I could fight so I found myself in the cages. I was good, too good, so they moved me into legitimate fights. The money was better for the family, you see?"

"I do."

Zel sighed and rubbed the back of his neck. "Matthias got his heart when he was nineteen months old. I was so happy. I couldn't stop crying when he finally woke up in that CVICU room. We had five really good years—and then he started having problems breathing and he was holding onto water and swelling. It was killing his kidneys. That's when I knew," he finished in a small voice. "That's when I knew my son was dying again."

"They couldn't get him another heart?" Sara could hardly breathe as she listened to Zel recount the heartbreaking loss of his son.

"He didn't survive the second transplant." Zel gulped loudly, and she could tell that he was on the verge of crying. Hating to see him in pain, she put her hand on his back and rubbed slow circles. Clearing his throat, Zel explained, "There's always a risk when a child undergoes bypass. The heart they gave him was strong and healthy—but his little body was tired." He exhaled roughly. "He was brain dead when they rolled him out of the operating room. It's a five percent chance. I kept hoping he would beat the odds a second time, but it didn't work out that way."

Sara didn't know what to say. She held tight to Zel's hand

as she tried to imagine what he had suffered.

"That little heart kept beating," he continued quietly. "I had to make a choice. I could let that heart—that gift—go with Matthias, or I could give another little boy or little girl a chance at life." He lifted his head, and there were unshed tears glimmering in his pale eyes. "I signed the papers, and I stayed with him until it was time for him to go into the operating room again. I broke down in that hospital room when he was gone—but that other father, the one whose little girl was going to live, came into the room and wrapped his arms around me. We cried together. Both of us. Grown men. Sobbing."

Overwhelmed by his sadness and grief, Sara embraced Zel. She didn't care about the plate that slid off her lap or the mess she was making. All she cared about was making sure this man who had just bared his soul to her felt the warmth and concern of another human being. It couldn't have been easy for him to make himself so vulnerable to her or recount what must have been the worst day of his life.

"Zel," she whispered while embracing him tightly. "I am so sorry that you lost your son." It wasn't nearly enough, but those were the only words that seemed appropriate.

He placed a gentle kiss on the side of her neck. "I shouldn't have poured all that out on you. I'm sorry."

Pulling back, she searched his handsome face. "Zel, please don't apologize. I'm honored that you felt safe enough with me to tell me about your son." Stroking his cheek, she asked, "What was he like?"

Zel smiled and cleared his throat. The sad haze in his eyes lifted as he remembered his little boy. "He was silly. He always laughing. He was never sad or grumpy. He was just the kindest, sweetest boy. He loved pirates and baseball, talked about them all the time."

"What did he look like?" She imagined a blond boy with icy blue eyes.

"His hair was darker than mine, like his mother's. He had blue eyes and freckles across his nose." He must have seen the curiosity in her face when he mentioned his son's mother because he explained, "We were never married. It was a very short relationship, and she left the hospital after Matthias was born. She couldn't handle it. She…wasn't well."

Carefully, Sara asked, "Does she know that he's gone?"

Zel shook his head. "She died three years ago. She was drinking, and she fell off a boat and drowned."

"That's awful."

"She was unwell. She had struggled with drinking and drugs, and I think she was consumed by guilt for leaving Matthias. I tried to keep in contact with her and made sure that she understood that she was always welcome in his life, but she wasn't ready for it." He sighed. "And then it was too late."

"You're very generous and very…adult about her," Sara remarked with some surprise. "Most people don't describe their exes or baby mamas and baby daddies that way."

Zel made a face. "I hate those names, and for better or worse, Anamarija and I were tied together through our son. I never told him that his mother had abandoned him or that she chose drugs and alcohol over him. He didn't need to know that."

"What did you tell him?"

"That she was sick and that she loved him more than anything in this world." Zel shrugged. "It was the truth. She loved our son, but she was sick." He eyed her in a way that made her uncomfortable. "And you? Why do I get the feeling that there's a dark secret in your past?"

"Because there is," she answered simply.

"Why do you dance?" Zel held tight to her hand, interlacing their fingers and keeping her close.

"I dance because I love to dance. I dance because I'm sexy as fuck and men want me," she answered boldly. "I dance because it helped me build a brand and a name that I'm using to sell millions of dollars of lingerie and clothing."

If he was impressed by that last part, he didn't show it. "But why did you start dancing?" Turning around her earlier question, he said, "You don't strike me as the kind of girl who dances. You're smart. You're ambitious. You obviously had other choices and options. So why dancing?"

"My family was hungry," she admitted with a no-bullshit look. "My dad was killed in a construction accident when I was kid. He was in the country illegally so he didn't have life insurance or anything. I was the oldest of 7 girls. When I was a senior in high school, Mom got hurt working in a shipping warehouse. I tried cleaning hotels and working as a waitress but it wasn't enough money."

"And then?"

"And then one day Besian walked into the steakhouse where I was working," she said. "When he was done with his meal, he told me I had a pretty face, great tits and a nice big ass and that there were plenty of men who would pay good money to see me dance."

Zel's eyes widened a bit, almost as if he might be offended

on her eighteen-year-old behalf. "And what did you say?"

"I told him he was a pig—but he left me a thousand dollar tip. Cash," she emphasized with a wry smile. "Crisp hundred dollar bills. I got that first taste of real money. It's hard to walk away from that so I decided to give it a try. I went to his club, and I auditioned and he put me on the main stage that first night. There was some kind of oil and gas conference in town and the men had deep pockets." The corners of her mouth twitched with amusement. "I made almost six thousand dollars in one night. I knew right then and there that if I was really smart I could do something amazing with my talent. I could *be* somebody."

"You don't have to make money to be somebody, Sara," he admonished gently. "You can be poor and be somebody that matters."

"I've been poor. It wasn't fun. I don't ever want to worry about money again. I don't ever want my mother or my sisters to worry about it either. I may be the one who dances and does the photoshoots and carries the brand, but this is a family business. My mother and my sisters are all involved with it— design, production, marketing, finance."

"And your stepbrother?"

"He has *nothing* to do with my business." Sara's stomach pitched with the mere mention of him. "He's usually in the pen anyway."

"Except for tonight," Zel insisted.

"Well I suspect he'll be headed right back there shortly," she said grimly. "He won't be able to stay out of trouble for very long. If my family is really lucky, he'll finally do something that gets him sent away forever."

"Why do you think he came here to bother you? Vegas is a long way from Houston."

An insistent knock echoed in the suite before Sara could answer. Shrugging, she rose to her feet to answer it. "I don't know why he's here. I don't really care. I just want him to go away."

"I don't think he's the kind of man who will go away quietly, Sara," Zel warned. Pointing at the door, he said, "Check the peep hole. There's always the chance he could be on the other side."

It was a slim chance, especially after she had spoken directly to the hotel's security and filed a report with the police, but Ramsay was a wily bastard. She peeked through the glass circle and spotted Lucy on the other side. Her sister had been fully aware that she intended to spend the night with Zel so she wasn't going to use her key to barge into the suite without knocking first.

Sara had barely opened the door when Lucy shoved it aside and announced, "I know why Ramsay is here." Panicked, she hurried into the penthouse. "Sarita, he's here because of your husband."

An invisible fist gripped her heart. In their family, they never referred to *him* by his real name. It was almost taboo to say it.

Husband.
That man.
The asshole.
The rat bastard.
The fucker who ruined your life.
But never his real name.

"Your *husband*?" Zel shot to his feet behind her. His face was a mask of shock and anger. "You're fucking *married*?"

"Shit," Lucy swore under her breath. "I'm sorry, Sara."

"Don't be sorry," Zel snarled angrily. "I'm glad someone thought I needed to know that the woman I just slept with is married!"

He disappeared into the bedroom and returned moments later with his shoes and belt in hand. "I'm leaving."

"Wait!" Sara tried to grab his hand as he stormed passed her. "Zel! Please."

Wordlessly, he jerked open the door and stepped into the hallway. Not willing to let him leave without explaining, she chased after him in only her lounging robe. "Zel, please, you have to let me explain!"

"What is there to explain, Sara?" He jabbed his finger at the elevator button. "You used me tonight. You made me complicit in your affair."

His accusation stung so badly. Angrily, she shouted, "My husband is Lalo Contreras."

The elevator dinged. The doors opened, but Zel didn't step inside the waiting car. He turned slowly and faced her, his expression now one of disbelief. "*You* are married to Lalo Contreras?"

Sara nodded slowly. "Yes. Officially. But we're separated."

"No, Sara," Lucy interrupted, "that's just it. You're not married anymore. You're a widow."

Sara spun around on her little sister. Incredulous, she asked, "What did you say?"

"You're a widow," Lucy repeated. "Lalo is dead."

For the first time in nine years, Sara felt free.

"He's…dead?"

Lucy nodded solemnly. "They found a body in a burned up motel. It was him."

Something in Zel's demeanor changed. Glancing around nervously, he stepped forward and grabbed her elbow. "We need to get inside right now. Don't say another word. Either of you."

Sara started to point out that the small foyer they were standing in was totally private, but she sensed that Zel knew more about Lalo's death. She allowed him to lead her inside the penthouse and secure the door. Turning around, he leaned back against it and said, "You both need to stop talking about Lalo's death in public. Keep it private—and leave it alone."

"What do you know?" Sara asked.

"I know that nothing good will come from digging into that night. Not unless you want to go up against Nikolai Kalasnikov, Besian and the cartel," he warned. As if trying to put together the pieces of a puzzle, he asked, "Why would your stepbrother come all this way to tell you that Lalo is dead? Why wouldn't he just call?"

Sara exchanged a nervous glance with her sister. Putting her trust in Zel, she said, "Everything Lalo owned is in my name. The houses, the cars, a few bank accounts…" Her voice faded as she watched Zel's expression morph to one of concern. "I know," she said quietly. "But in my defense, I was just a nineteen-year-old kid who was stupidly in love with the boy-next-door."

As if aware of the sensitive discussion about to happen, Lucy quickly excused herself to her bedroom on the opposite end of the suite. Stepping toward Zel, Sara touched his hand

and captured his gaze. "Will you please let me explain?"

He didn't hesitate. "Yes."

Taking his hand, she guided him to the bedroom where they had made love only hours earlier. She sat down on the bed, scooting back across the rumpled sheets until her back touched the piles of pillows that had been hastily tossed aside, and Zel sat in front of her. "I'm sorry that I didn't tell you that I am—*was*—legally married. I am—*was*—separated. We lived separate lives in separate towns and had nothing to do with each other."

"Why didn't you divorce him?"

She laughed harshly. "You seem to know Lalo. You must know what he's like. There was no way in hell he was going to let me go. I tried to get free. I offered him more money each year, but he wouldn't sign the papers. It was about control. It was *always* about control with him."

"Why would you marry a monster like that?" Zel seemed incapable of comprehending how she could have chosen someone like Lalo.

Pinching the hem of her robe between her forefinger and thumb, she began her tale. "I was just a kid, Zel. I was young and dumb and in love. Lalo was from my neighborhood. We grew up together. We had dated while I was in high school so there was already history and a pull there. We started hanging out again and then dating and before I knew it we were standing in a courthouse getting married."

"How old were you?"

"Nineteen," she said, "and he was twenty-one. We loved each other." Zel made a face, and she insisted, "Lalo did love me, but his version of love wasn't the same as mine. It was controlling and possessive. He got crazy and dangerous. He made me stop dancing—which caused problems with Besian, as I'm sure you can imagine."

"I can imagine," he echoed flatly.

"Within six months, our marriage had imploded. I went back to the house I shared with my mom and sisters, and he stayed in the house we had bought together as a married couple."

"The house in your name," he amended.

She nodded. "I had more money than him back then. I would give him half of everything I earned, and he used it to bring in more product that he turned around and sold on the streets. It made him very popular with the cartel, and he grew fast. Maybe too fast," she said, thinking of his paranoia and his hunger for power.

Exhaling roughly, she recalled, "When I went back to work for Besian, Lalo fucking lost it. He went into the club where I was dancing and started attacking patrons. He had his crew with him. They trashed the place. When Besian got there with his men, it was mayhem. Blood. Glass. Broken chairs. Busted up doors. And then? Gunshots."

"Shit."

"It was awful. The police showed up, of course. Everyone ended up in jail that night." She rubbed her face between her hands. "Nikolai showed up at my house. This was back in his early days in Houston when he was really dangerous. From what I've heard, he's mellowed out a lot and is more into legit business now. Back then?" She shuddered. "You didn't want to come face-to-face with him. It was bad enough if he sent Alexei or Ivan or—God forbid—Kostya to deal with you."

"What did he want?"

"He told me to sort my shit out—or he would sort me out." She gulped at the memory. "To him, I was just some stupid girl causing problems. I didn't want to go back to Lalo, but I didn't have any choice. For me, going back to Besian and dancing was just about business and earning a living. To him? It was a slap in the face. It was about his wife—his woman—choosing to dance naked for an Albanian loan shark. He was going to start a war to save face, and Nikolai wasn't going to let that happen. It was pretty clear that Kostya was going to make me disappear if I didn't make things right with my husband."

"What happened when you went back?"

Sara couldn't meet Zel's intense gaze. Dropping her focus to her hands, she wrung them together and tried not to dredge up the memories threatening to surface. "Lalo wasn't happy. He decided I needed to be taught a lesson. He made sure it was one I wouldn't forget."

Very gently, Zel reached out and traced the bridge of her nose. "Was that when this happened?" At her look of surprise, he smiled sadly. "In my business, you get to know the signs of a broken and healed nose." He studied her face a moment longer and then traced the apple of her left cheek and the slant of her jaw. "And these?"

She nodded, her eyes stinging as the memories of horrific pain surfaced. "It was a long three nights tied up in that trap house before Alexei Sarnov bailed Besian out of jail so Besian could come looking for me."

"Besian saved you?" Zel seemed taken aback. "Even after all the trouble you'd caused him?"

"Besian has his faults, but he's loyal to his friends. No mat-

ter what happened with Lalo, he was never going to abandon
me."

"So what happened when he found you?"

"He nearly killed Lalo. The two slingers he was letting take
turns with me?" She drew a slow line across her neck. "By
morning, most of Lalo's crew had vanished, and he was in Ben
Taub's ICU."

"And you?"

"Besian had Alexei get me out of Houston. He drove me to
Dallas and put me in a hotel there to wait."

"For?"

"For Besian to fix things with Nikolai," she said simply.

"Is that why you have that tattoo?"

She nodded and touched the fading mark. "Besian gave up
part of his territory and had to give two of his clubs to Kostya.
The dollar figure was so high I didn't know if I would ever pay
it off."

"But you did."

"I did." She nodded. "Besian and Alexei—he'd been one of
my favorite patrons—gave me some seed money for my
lingerie company idea. I knew that the only way I could turn
that company into a reality was to create a sexy as fuck plus-
sized personality. A brand," she emphasized. "I created this
Nena Rubens character and learned how to leverage social
media. I came to Vegas to dance and learn and network. I
started a burlesque show that traveled to New York and Los
Angeles and San Francisco. *That's* when I launched the
lingerie and other products. I waited until I had a hungry
audience and then I pounced. As long as my family was
supported, I didn't care about a salary for myself. I paid Besian

and Alexei back first—with interest—and then plowed my cut back into the business until we were turning a serious profit."

"And now you're doing very well," he finished for her.

"Very well."

Almost reluctantly, Zel asked, "Why is your stepbrother here now? What does he think he's going to gain by harassing you?"

She cringed before admitting, "He took the heat for the gunshots that night Lalo stormed Besian's club. He went to prison for it. When he got out, Lalo cut him loose and refused to bring him back into the family. When Ramsay wouldn't stop causing problems, he set him up and had him sent back to prison. It was a huge betrayal. I'm sure that Ramsay thinks he's owed what I've just inherited. Houses, cars, bank accounts—Lalo put most of it in my name. He was a dick, but he always kept my credit clean so he could use it whenever he needed it."

"You can't touch the bank accounts or the houses or the cars," Zel warned. "You know the DEA and the FBI and the Texas Rangers will be all over that shit. You need a lawyer. A good one," he emphasized. "This might be a good time to call in any favors you can from Besian. If anyone knows how to stay on the right side of the law, it's him."

"I'm sure he'll be contacting me soon." She was baffled as to why he hadn't contacted her already. It occurred to her that something even worse than Lalo's death must have happened back in Houston for Besian to have overlooked a simple phone call. She didn't even want to imagine what that might be.

As if reading her thoughts, Zel said, "Don't ask those questions, Sara. You're smart enough to know what happens to people who know too much. Whoever killed Lalo must have been protected from high above. You don't need that shadow following you around, baby."

She glanced at him with surprise as the tender name he'd used. It was a glimpse at the future, of a possibility of something serious with this man who had shared his secrets and learned hers.

Still guilt-ridden, she clasped his hand. "Zel, I'm so sorry I didn't tell you that I was married. I haven't considered myself married in years. I've had zero contact with Lalo. We were living separate lives. It was only legal papers keeping us tied together." She bit her lip. "But you were right to feel angry about my lie. I wouldn't like it very much if I found out you were married."

Zel grasped the back of her neck and brushed his thumb along the sensitive spot behind her ear. "I understand why you kept that secret. I didn't appreciate being blindsided by it, but I won't hold that against you."

"Thank you."

Ever so slowly, his hand drifted down her leg and picked up her foot. As he massaged her instep, the air between them grew heavy with sexual tension. "Would you like me to stay?"

"Yes." She wanted him to stay and never leave. Tonight. Tomorrow. For as long as he wanted to be with her.

"I'll keep you safe, Sara. I won't let Ramsay touch you again."

She understood the weight of that vow. This was a man who had survived a staggering amount of grief and pain. This was a man who was going to step into a cage into two nights and take punishing punches and kicks to make things right with the mobsters who owned him because he had given his word.

As he crawled toward her like a cat on the prowl, Sara wondered what the hell she was getting herself into now. When their lips met, she shoved aside all those trifling thoughts and focused only on the excitement fluttering in her belly.

Tomorrow. I'll deal with the reality tomorrow.

CHAPTER FIVE

THE HIGH-PITCHED WHIR of a jump rope whined in Zel's ears. His feet moved quickly on the mat while his wrists flicked the rope, sometimes switching up the rhythm.

Normally he'd have been jumping at an ever-faster pace but he was dragging ass this afternoon. Between his night with Sara and the final push of cutting weight before the upcoming weigh-in, his energy level was less than optimal. Luckily, when he'd stepped on the scale upon arriving in Vegas five days earlier, he had only been seven pounds overweight after being on a strict pre-cut regimen. His bounce back starting tonight and tomorrow wouldn't beat his body to hell.

Rumor had it that his opponent was tipping the scales over twenty-six pounds high. Mace had been fighting in the light heavyweight class for years, but he'd recently made the move to the next lower class in a bid for dominance and an advantage in the cage. It was a risk for a fighter that heavy and that big to go down a class, but Mace clearly felt he had no other choice. His career was played out in his division. He needed to make this new class work—or else his days fighting for money were over.

Ivan's training philosophies didn't include pushing his fighters to compete in weight classes so far outside their natural body sizes. He didn't allow the fighters on his roster too get fat or out of shape in between fights either. He wanted them all within ten to fifteen pounds of their fighting class and eating clean most of the time. He had different ideas about long-term strength and endurance than many of his peers.

Some training camps encouraged—demanded—their fighters drop twenty or more pounds in a fight week and then gain all that weight back within twenty-four hours of their match. It was supposed to be a way to ensure a competitive edge over an opponent but it was fraught with risk.

Dehydration was no joke. Fighters suffered terribly. The huge swings of weight loss and weight gain were hell on the body and the mind. With the brain so dried up from the lack of fluids, it banged around in the skull with every hit and made the risk of serious concussions very high. He had known men who ended up in the hospital with serious heart issues after all the diuretics, caffeine, saunas and hot baths forced on them during the cut. Mixed-martial arts was dangerous enough without adding the strain of extreme weight loss.

Zel should have been concentrating on the weigh-in set to start in a few hours, but he couldn't shake Sara from his mind. The tangled mess her late husband had left behind was a quagmire he shouldn't wade into, but he couldn't help himself. He should have run the other way the second he heard the name Lalo Contreras, but he couldn't do it.

After a single night with Sara and a morning waking up with her in secure in his arms, he was totally and completely twisted up in her. Her delicious taste, her tantalizing smell—she hadd invaded his senses and taken hold. Zel wondered if he would ever escape the infatuation.

Do I even want to escape it?

His stomach rolled with heat at the memory of those thick thighs wrapped around his head. He could almost taste her. Her shrieks of pleasure echoed in his ears. He remembered the debauched expression on her face as he'd kissed his way up her belly afterward and—

He tripped on the rope and tumbled forward. "Shit!"

With that booming voice, Ivan shouted angrily as he surged across the gym floor. He let loose a string of swear words, jumbling together Russian, Albanian, Croatian, Spanish and English in a colorful way that would have been impressive if it hadn't been directed at him. Snarling, Ivan demanded, "Get your mind off that pussy and on your foot work!"

Cringing at the public scolding, Zel unwound the rope from his ankle and stood. Abashed, he offered an apologetic smile. "Sorry, Ivan."

"I don't want to hear sorry. I want to see you focused! You lose your focus and you get hurt."

Nodding contritely, Zel cleared his mind and focused on his routine. If Sara could affect him this badly after one night, he probably needed to steer clear until after his fight. He couldn't risk any distractions, not with so much riding on the line. He desperately needed the prize money to satisfy his obligations.

But winning money wasn't the reason Ivan had been riding him so hard in preparation for this fight. Ivan wanted him to be free of his debt, but his coach was more concerned about safety. Last year, Mace had killed a man in the ring with a vicious yet legal blow to the head. Zel tried not to dwell on it but the reality of the danger of stepping into the ring with Mace was very genuine. One misstep, one diversion—and he could be paralyzed or dead.

No. There was absolutely no room for error or distraction.

Or Sara.

That thought made him uncomfortable as he headed into the sauna. Even now he craved her. His willpower and determination had brought him this far in his life, but saying no to Sara? He wasn't so sure.

And he'd promised to keep her safe. He had already made a personal visit down to the hotel's security to ask them to be even more vigilant with her. A few signed autographs and fight night passes had been enough to ensure that she would be safe in the hotel. Outside on the streets of Vegas was another story. It would be so easy for a man like Ramsay to snatch her.

And then I'll have to kill him...

The thought stampeded through his brain. It wasn't an empty or dramatic thought. It was simply the truth. He wasn't an underworld player. He didn't live in the seedy underbelly of Houston. Yet, given the choice between letting Ramsay hurt Sara or taking him out, he wouldn't hesitate or flinch. Her stepbrother was clearly a man who wasn't afraid of the police or the law. He would hurt her and her family unless someone stopped him.

Eyes closed, head resting against the wall of the sauna, he breathed in the heated air and tried to fight that claustrophobic sensation gripping his gut. Whether it came from the thought of spilling blood to protect a woman he hardly knew or the damp and nearly unbearable heat surrounding him, he couldn't tell. Breathing deeply, he reminded himself he only needed a short time in here today.

The door to the sauna opened, and Zel cracked an eyelid. He watched Ivan stride into the sauna, a crisp white towel tight around his waist. There was hardly an inch of Ivan's skin that wasn't covered in ink. Each tattoo told a part of Ivan's story, each slash of blue or black ink another hint at the life of violence and crime he had lived.

Well—maybe not all of them. Zel zeroed in on the newer pieces decorating his coach's body. They were all for Erin and told a different story, a story of something new and bright and filled with hope. He suspected those tattoos were Ivan's version of love notes for his beloved wife.

Ivan had always loved a good steam room so Zel wasn't surprised to see him in here today. There was a look on Ivan's face that made him wary. Certain he was about to get an earful of advice and criticism from his coach, he steeled himself for the worst.

Ivan surprised him by chuckling darkly as he settled onto the bench and stretched out his legs. "You aren't going to believe the phone call I just had."

Zel's chest tightened as he imagined all sorts of scenarios. Was it Besian telling Ivan that Lalo Contreras was dead? Was it Nikolai warning Ivan that shit was about to go down with Sara? Was the cartel headed this way to pressure Sara into giving them Lalo's assets? Were the Feds coming here to shake her down and make trouble?

"Lyosha is here."

Zel shrugged as he idly scratched his chest. Alexei coming to Vegas was nothing strange or out of the ordinary, certainly nothing to warrant the surprise on Ivan's face. "He always comes to Vegas for his birthday."

"He didn't come alone. He brought that pretty little maid of his and took her straight to the courthouse." Ivan paused for dramatic effect. "He's going to marry her. Tonight."

Shocked, Zel glanced back at Ivan. "Did you know it was that serious?"

"It had to be serious for him to stick his neck out like that for her," Ivan answered matter-of-factly.

"The way you stuck your neck out for Erin?"

"The way you're going to stick your neck out for Sara Contreras," Ivan shot back with a knowing glance.

"Running off Sara's stepbrother is nothing compared to the things you did for Erin or the things Alexei has done for the cleaning lady."

"If you hang around Sara long enough, you'll have to do the same things I did for Erin," Ivan warned. "Maybe even worse."

Because he needed advice and Ivan was the only man qualified to give it, Zel blurted out, "Lalo is dead."

Ivan's expression slackened. "Dead? You're sure?"

Zel nodded. "That's why Ramsay is in town. He seems to think he's owed everything that Sara has just inherited."

Ivan made a face. "That's bad news, Zel. She's going to have the DEA, FBI, the Texas Rangers and everyone else digging through her life. You don't need that kind of shit in your life."

He understood what Ivan was saying without saying it. If they were dating and the Feds started looking at Sara, they would start digging into his history. They might uncover things that men like Besian would rather keep hidden.

With a rough exhale, Ivan declared, "There is a lot of history with that woman that you don't know."

"She told me everything last night." He glanced back at Ivan and met his coach's hard gaze. "Everything. Besian. The dancing. Her marriage to Lalo. The drug deals. The fight at Besian's club. Alexei bailing Besian out and hiding her away in Dallas after Besian rescued her. They money they gave her for her business." He touched the mark that mirrored his on his own skin. "Her tattoo."

"What she didn't tell you is the things she doesn't know that went down that night of the club attack," Ivan grumbled. "She was this close," he held his thick finger and thumb only a few centimeters apart, "from the end." He slashed his hand across the front of his throat. "She's lucky that so many people liked her and spoke up for her, but there's still bad blood between her and Nikolai. She'll never be allowed back in Houston."

It was a subtle warning about possible future complications. Unbothered by it, Zel replied, "I'm not tied to Houston anymore. Not after tomorrow night."

"If you win," Ivan reminded him carefully.

"I'm going to win." There was no other possibility in Zel's mind. He had visualized the fight hundreds of times, thousands even. He was going to win—and then he was going to walk away a free man.

And maybe, if he was very lucky, he would be walking away with Sara right next to him.

"You better win." Ivan stretched his arms high overhead and inhaled deeply. "If you don't, Erin is going to have my ass when she finds out how much I have in Besian's book for this fight."

Zel pretended not to hear that. Illegal gambling with a known mobster would get them both in deep shit with the league.

"Alexei wants you at the wedding tonight. It's at the Bellagio. I'll text you the details when I get them."

"I'll be there." He and Alexei had been friends since his first day in Houston. Alexei had been the one to help him find a cheap apartment close to the hospital and odd jobs to make ends meet.

"I told Alexei that Sara is in town. She'll get an invite so you two may as well come together."

An irrational flare of jealousy burned Zel as he remembered Sara's story from last night. She had mentioned Alexei giving her seed money. Knowing what he did of Alexei's reputation with dancing girls, he had to ask, "Sara and Alexei…?"

Ivan laughed and smacked Zel's shoulder hard enough to knock him off balance. "No. Never. Not like that." Smiling, Ivan added, "Alexei tried, but she wasn't having it. They're friends. That's it."

He felt like an asshole to be so relieved by Ivan's assertion. Whatever Sara had done in her past life was none of his business—but he'd be a liar if he said that the thought of her in bed with Alexei hadn't twisted up his insides.

"She was young when she made her mistakes." Ivan closed his eyes and leaned his head back against the wall of the sauna. "We were all fuck-ups at that age. She's done right by her family and her friends. She squared things with Besian and Alexei. Hell," Ivan exhaled a long, slow breath, "I'm sure if she asked nicely, Nikolai would lift his banishment and welcome her back into the city. We've all moved on since then."

"I'm ready to move on," Zel said, the thought coming to him suddenly. It might have been the dehydration and heat, but he felt giddy and lightheaded. "I'm ready to start living again."

Ivan eyed him closely. "If she made you wake up and want to live again after one night in her bed, she must know some special tricks."

Zel shot him the finger, and Ivan laughed.

More serious now, Ivan said, "That's good, Zel. It's very good. You need to live. Your little boy was so special. He was such a good kid. He was always happy and smiling, and— forgive me—but I think he wouldn't like to see you this way. Sad. Withdrawn. Alone." He shook his head. "I was alone for too long. If Erin hadn't come into the gym that day, I would still be a miserable, lonely bastard. She changed my life, and I'm a lucky man for that. If Sara can do that for you? Let her."

Ivan's advice rattled around in his head as Zel finished up his time in the sauna, took a long shower and then stepped on the scale. He was three pounds under the limit for the middle-weight class. Pleased, he stepped off and went in search of a bottle of water. He sipped it slowly, just enough to wet his mouth, and moved to a quiet, relaxed corner of the locker room to wait.

After the highly publicized weigh-in at six o'clock, he would have just enough time to change into a suit and head to the Bellagio for Alexei's wedding. He wouldn't be able to stay long after the ceremony. He needed to rehydrate and start fueling his body for the grueling contest that awaited him.

"Here." Ivan waved a cell phone. "Your phone was ringing in your locker."

Zel caught it and glanced at the screen. He had a missed call from Sara and had a text message waiting. He swiped his thumb over the screen and tapped in his code so he could read it.

I'm sure you've heard the good news! No better way to spend a Friday night than a Vegas wedding! <3 <3 <3

His thumb hesitated over the screen of his phone. He wasn't good at flirting via text. Hell, he wasn't very skilled when it came to flirting in person. He finally tapped out a message and hit send, all the while hoping she would say yes.

Spend your Friday night with me? Weigh-in. Wedding. Dinner.

He tapped his phone against his thigh while he anxiously awaited her reply. It came a few minutes later.

Yes!

Smiling like a fool, he typed back a quick message, letting her know that he would make sure her name was on the VIP seat list for the weigh-in and then escort her to the wedding at the Bellagio.

"Hey, it's time." Ivan rapped his knuckles on a locker to get Zel's attention.

Inhaling a deep breath, he set aside his phone and got dressed. It was a short walk to the holding rooms where each fighter and his team waited for their turn to walk onto the stage for the televised weigh-in. After the weigh-in, he would have time to change into his suit for the presser that would follow. Once that was done, his obligations to the league were completed for the night.

And then Sara is all mine...

Feeling those pre-fight jitters, Zel stretched his neck as he waited for the elevator to reach their floor. He was already in his walkout gear, his T-shirt and trunks nearly skin-tight and emblazoned with the Markovic MMA logo as well as the various brands who paid to promote him and the league. He hated these weigh-in spectacles. The pressure to perform for the cameras had never been something he enjoyed. He liked to brawl in the cage. He was good at that part.

But this? Posing aggressively? The trash talk? It just wasn't his style. He wanted to walk onstage, step on the scale and walk right off, but he couldn't. The contracts he had signed demanded that he play the part—and so he would.

When the elevator reached their floor, he followed Ivan and the other trainers on his team. He glanced across the hall just in time to see Sara come into view. A black dress hugged her curves, accentuating the fullness of her breasts and that luscious ass he had worshipped last night. Surrounded by her entourage, she walked toward the weigh-in room to take her VIP seat.

Their eyes met across the crowded lobby and instantly the sparks of desire ignited his lust. A gaggle of her fans stepped into the way, thrusting cell phones at her in search of the perfect selfie and momentarily obstructing his view. Zel slowed his pace as he crossed the distance between them. She'd just finished smiling for the last photo when he neared her.

As they passed, Zel was so close he caught the bright citrus scent of her perfume. Briefly, Sara's fingers touched his. Paper crinkled against his skin. Without looking down, Zel accepted her note, the giddy nervousness of his schoolboy days suddenly fresh in his mind. He didn't dare glance at his hand, afraid to alert anyone to the note she'd just passed.

Fist clenched, he followed Ivan without breaking step. It was only when he reached the safety of the holding room with the rest of his team that he uncurled his fingers and looked at the note in his hand. The folded slip of paper held a perfect lip print in the sexiest shade of red.

Suddenly, he couldn't stop imagining all the places he wanted her to leave lip prints like that. His mind refused to focus on the task at hand. Even when it was his turn to weigh-in, he was consumed by thoughts of Sara and the night ahead of them. He was oblivious to the cameras or the promoters and even his opponent. He peeled out of his walkout shirt, stepped up to the scale—and spotted Sara sitting right there in the front row.

Wickedly sexy, Sara flashed a playful smile and wink. His groin tightened and he prayed he wasn't about to sport wood right here in front of everyone. It would be a press photo he would never live down.

Across the stage, he met Mace's cold stare. His opponent looked like hell. The usually bulky fighter was now ripped so lean his skin looked drawn and tight. Every sinewy cord was visible in the other man's neck and arms. Cutting all that weight had reduced him to his leanest state, but he seemed glassy eyed and almost confused.

As he stepped on the scale, Zel locked eyes with Sara. They shared a sizzling glance, and his heart thumped wildly in his chest. He gulped and broke eye contact. The professional fighter within him urged common sense and reminded him that he needed a clear head and rest for tomorrow night's fight.

But the red-blooded man within him, the primal side that drove him inside the ring, had other ideas. Dirty, sexy, sweaty, all-night until they both collapsed ideas.

Suddenly, Mace wasn't his biggest worry anymore. He would win this fight if he relied on his innate talent and trusted the skills he had honed under Ivan's watchful eye.

No, his biggest concern was Sara. One night with this woman, and he was ready to live again. There was something about her that made him feel invincible—and that was dangerous, especially with the hardest fight of his career and threat of her stepbrother looming just out of sight.

If I'm not careful, she's going to be the death of me.

The thought didn't scare him nearly as much as it should have.

CHAPTER SIX

S ARA COULDN'T BELIEVE her first real date with Zel was a wedding! She wasn't sure if that was supposed to be good luck or bad luck. Considering her track record with men, she decided she had probably unwittingly doomed her relationship with Zel by agreeing to come as his date.

But Alexei was like family to her, a man who had been something of an older brother for the past ten years, and she wasn't about to miss out on such a wonderful moment in his life. During their short phone call earlier that afternoon, she hadn't gotten much out of him about the identity of his bride, just her first name and the story of how he had met her. It seemed like a sweet romance, and she was happy for Alexei.

Standing at the front of the Bellagio's beautifully decorated east chapel, Alexei exuded confidence and power in his crispy pressed and cleanly tailored dark suit. Ivan stood next to him in a similar dark suit and seemed to be giving Alexei last-minute advice. Ivan was probably one of the few men that Alexei would actually listen to when it came to women so she hoped Ivan was giving him some useful pointers for navigating the ups and downs of marriage.

From what Sara had heard from friends back in Houston, Ivan had settled down very happily into marital bliss. A few rows ahead of Sara, Erin Markovic looked stunning in a cobalt blue cocktail dress with a fantastic black belt that nipped in her already tiny waist and accentuated her fit curves. By the looks of it, Ivan had finally found someone he enjoyed spoiling with lavish gifts. Diamonds dangled from her ears and glinted around her neck. The rock on her left hand was slightly bigger than the diamond she wore on her right.

Yet the tender smile on Erin's face anytime she looked at her husband was enough to convince Sara that theirs was a match based on true love and deep devotion. Sara remembered Ivan from his early days in Houston. Back then, the Russian brute was known for violence and mayhem. He was the man who never questioned the orders that came from Nikolai and did whatever was necessary to grow their territory and gain more control over the city.

Despite that hard reputation, he had never been unkind toward women. That seemed to be his line in the sand. Once, he had come into Besian's club Harem, the spot where she had started her career, with Alexei. She still remembered how uncomfortable he had looked and how quickly he had lumbered out of that club and disappeared. Maybe even all those years ago he had been looking for something a little different than his peers.

It seemed that he had found what he was looking for in Erin. She reminded Sara of a ballerina with her slim build and graceful way of moving. Apparently that saying about opposites attracting had some truth to it because she had never seen two people who were more different—or so obviously happy.

"I didn't think I was going to make it."

Sara glanced to her right at the unexpected sound of Besian's familiar voice. He gestured to the open space next to her in the pew before sliding into it. Unbuttoning his suit jacket, he flashed her a smile and then leaned forward so he could make eye contact with Zel. They exchanged a brief glance before Zel turned his attention to the front of the chapel. She didn't fault him for the public display of coldness toward Besian. The last thing he needed was someone digging around and trying to publicly tie him to a known mob boss with his dirty hands wrist-deep in loans and gambling.

"It's a good thing I have friends with access to private jets. There wasn't a seat left on any of the Houston flights coming to Vegas. I had to make a deal with the devil for my seat," he said, brushing lint from his pants. "The things I do for my friends!"

She caught his double-meaning in the sly look he directed toward her. Leaning closer, she asked in a whisper, "When were you going to tell me about *him*?"

"*That* is a conversation I wasn't prepared to have over the phone or via email or text." He checked his phone for any messages and switched it to silent before tucking it back into his pocket. "We'll discuss that later tonight."

"Tomorrow," she corrected, a faint blush making her face hot. "I have plans."

Besian eyed Zel's hand as it moved to her thigh, just above her knee, in a gentle but clearly possessive gesture. That seemed to be Zel's unspoken way of telling Besian that the rules were different now.

"I see," Besian replied with a hint of a smile. "I can't wait to hear the story behind that." As he fetched a jawbreaker from his pocket, he glanced back to see the last few guests trickling into the room. He made a grumbling sound before popping the candy into his mouth. Voice lowered, he murmured, "Stay close to me tonight until I smooth things over with our old friend."

Barely moving her neck, Sara looked toward the aisle of the chapel and felt her heart flutter in her chest when Nikolai Kalasnikov and his very pregnant wife came into view. He looked every bit the mafia don in that black suit and black tie. The dark ink marking his fingers was plainly visible, and at this distance, she could see the little bit of ink that even his shirt collars didn't cover. Beneath that designer suit, Nikolai's body was rumored to be a canvas of criminal and mafia ink, each piece recording his violent history and rise to power.

As if sensing her presence, Nikolai glanced to the right. His gaze skipped from Besian's face to hers. His expression remained stoic and unmoving. There was only the briefest hint of recognition in his eyes before he returned his attention to Alexei. She swallowed anxiously at the mob boss's dismissal of her. She hadn't even warranted a frown. Surely that meant he wasn't going to order Alexei to toss her out of the chapel—or worse.

Apparently unaware of the history that her husband had with Sara, Vivian smiled warmly at Besian and touched his upper arm before locking eyes with Sara and smiling again. Sara had come face-to-face with many beautiful women during her years of modeling and dancing but Nikolai's wife was that kind of beautiful that belonged in a global glossy ad campaign for something like Cover Girl or Maybelline. She was *that* pretty.

She knew how to dress, choosing a black cocktail dress

with a champagne pink bodice peeking through a delicate lace overlay, and accentuated her good looks with makeup. A smoky eye with a hint of shimmer. Lush red lips. A hint of blush. She'd mastered the art of hot rollers to achieve those incredible dark waves. Her jewelry choices were classic and understated, but Sara had an eye for diamonds and Vivian was wearing the absolute best.

When Vivian tugged on Nikolai's hand to guide him to the bride's mostly empty side of the chapel, she confirmed the rumors Sara had heard about her sweet nature. She was obviously thinking about how Alexei's bride would feel with all those empty pews. Sara had been wondering why those pews were so light on occupants. It was clear Alexei's wedding had been something of a rush. There were only three reasons Sara could think of to explain it.

One: Alexei was so desperately in love with this woman that he couldn't wait even three days for a license and a quickie courthouse wedding in Houston.

Two: His soon-to-be bride was pregnant, and he wanted to assure her that he was excited about a baby and building a life with her.

Three: Something had happened—something dangerous to her or him or both of them—that necessitated an immediate marriage to protect them from the legal implications.

Or, maybe, it was all three.

After Vivian and Nikolai settled onto the front pew, Vivian said something to her husband who gave the smallest, almost imperceptible shake of his head. He slid his arm around his wife's shoulders, and she leaned into him. Nikolai pressed a loving kiss to the top of her head. It was jarring for

Sara to see the man who had terrified her almost ten years ago showing such tenderness.

"He's as soft as a kitten these days," Besian joked while tucking the jawbreaker wrapper into his pocket.

Zel grunted and said, "Even kittens can scratch."

Besian chuckled as the soft tones of the ceremonial music filled the room. They stood with the rest of the guests and watched as the maid of honor, a platinum blonde in a delicate lace dress the color of a shell pink cameo, walked down the aisle. She took her place at the front of the chapel and turned back to watch the bride make her entrance.

Sara peeked around Besian to get a good look at the woman who had won Alexei's heart—and she inhaled a sharp breath of recognition. Alexei had mentioned that his bride-to-be's name was Shay, but Sara had never imagined that he meant Shay Sandoval, Shannon's little sister!

Except she wasn't so little anymore.

In the nine years since Sara had last seen her, Shay had blossomed into a stunning beauty. Sara had been very good friends with Shannon, especially since their men had run in the same street gang back then. Shannon and Ruben had been a few years younger than Sara and Lalo. Once, after one of Lalo's more vicious attacks, she had tried to convince Shannon to get out of the life while she could. She hadn't listened back then and Sara had a sickening feeling that Shannon was still running with her man, a true ride-or-die chica.

But Shay had always been such a good kid, so smart and ambitious and kind. Sara had been sure Shay was going places. Seeing Shay as a confident, poised young woman left Sara with all sorts of questions. Namely, where the hell was Shannon?

As if reading her mind, Besian caught her eye. There was something in his face that unsettled her. The timing of Alexei's wedding and the news about Lalo had seemed like a coincidence to her but maybe it wasn't. Shay was such a pretty young thing, and Lalo had always been fond of a certain type. Shannon was probably still up to her eyes in the street gang life with Ruben which meant Shay, who had always been such a good girl, would have been right in front of Lalo all the time. He would have wanted to ruin and hurt her the same way he had Sara.

Unless Alexei had stepped in to save her...

What had Alexei said on the phone? That Shay had worked with a commercial cleaning company that serviced his dealerships? Sara could imagine the two of them dancing around each other for weeks or months while their shared attraction grew and strengthened. For all his bluster about mistresses and the weakness of love, Alexei had always struck Sara as the kind of man who desperately wanted a wife and children, a family to love and support and pamper and give all the things he had been denied as a child and young man.

Apparently he had recognized those same desires in Shay. Shay who had been abused by her terrible mother and the disgusting men she had brought home with her and who had been abandoned and left with only Shannon as a parental figure. If Alexei had fallen for Shay and Lalo had tried to hurt her? Oh, shit. Lalo never would have stood a chance.

Sara felt Shay's surprised gaze settling on her. She smiled warmly at the beautiful bride, and Shay beamed right back at her before continuing her walk down the aisle to Alexei. When she reached the front of the chapel, she handed her gorgeous bouquet of pink and white flowers to her maid of honor. Alexei grasped both of her hands in his, being extra careful with the one wrapped in gauze, and gazed down at his soon-to-be-wife with such love that Sara found herself blinking rapidly. All she had ever wanted was for a man to look at her like that, as if his entire world was wrapped up in her.

Zel's strong fingers wrapped around hers as they took their seats. She glanced at him and experienced a heated thrill that rushed through her body. Zel intense look wasn't one of lust or desire. It was something more, something better, something deeper. He was looking at her as if he could see a future with her. She witnessed the promise of something far greater than two wild nights in Vegas when she stared into his eyes.

Rattled by the realization that Zel might be the man she had been looking for all this time, she clung to his hand and tried not to smile too much while Alexei and Shay recited their vows and exchanged rings. She ignored the guilty sensation pricking the edges of her conscience as she sat there happy and dreaming of all the possibilities Zel seemed to be offering while her husband was cold and stiff on a morgue slab in Houston. The relief she had experienced upon learning Lalo was dead and could never hurt her again had bothered her all day. Even if her husband had been the world's worst human being, it didn't seem right to rejoice at his death.

You're still letting him control your emotions. The thought struck her suddenly. As if he were still alive, Lalo's ghost was manipulating her feelings. *No more, Sara. He's gone. Let it go.*

Zel gave her hand a squeeze as Alexei and Shay sealed their wedding vows with an excited kiss. Holding tight to his hand, she stood with Zel, only letting go to applaud the smiling newlyweds. When Alexei and Shay walked back down the aisle, Zel slipped his arm around her waist and gave her hip a pat. She leaned back into him and relished the powerful wall of heat and strength that supported her. He brushed his lips against her temple, and Sara damn near swooned right there in that chapel.

After the wedding party moved down the aisle, everyone seemed to wait for Nikolai and Vivian to leave their pew first. Besian followed next and then the remainder of the guests—Erin Markovic and a bunch of single men who were either fighters from the gym or friends of Alexei's—trailed after him. Sara took Zel's offered arm and let him escort her out of the chapel and into the small reception area where the newlyweds were receiving their congratulations.

When it was their turn, she tightly embraced Alexei. "I am so happy for you."

He hugged her back, one of his arms noticeable stronger than the other. "Thank you. It's so good to see you here."

Stepping back, Sara grinned at Shay. "I'm not sure if you remember me...?"

"I remember you, Sara," Shay confirmed with a pleased smile.

A hugger by nature, Sara embraced Shay and wished her the very best in her new married life with Alexei. "I think he's very lucky to have won your heart."

"I think we're both very lucky," Shay replied softly while sharing a secret glance with her husband. Something dark flitted across her face, a memory or a thought, and Shay blinked away the shimmering evidence of unshed tears. "I wish Shannon was here, Sara. I think she'd really like to talk you."

Sara wanted to ask why Shannon was missing from her baby sister's wedding, but the haunted and sad glint to Shay's dark eyes warned her not to go there. The bandage on Shay's hand and the way Alexei seemed to be favoring that one arm sent Sara's imagination into overdrive. She might have been imagining it, but Sara thought she could even see the faintest hint of a bruise on Shay's neck.

Knowing what she did of Houston's underworld, it wasn't hard to piece all those clues together. Someone had tried to hurt Shay, and Alexei had reacted as any man with his idea of honor and loyalty and love would and had been injured in the process.

And if Lalo had been the man who put his hands on Shay...?

Zel gave her arm a little squeeze, and they moved down the very short reception line. When he steered her to the left, Nikolai stepped in front of her. He was taller than she had remembered and leaner. He might have softened his heart when it came to his wife, but Sara recognized that dangerous spark in his green eyes. This was not a man to be crossed.

Holding her breath, she waited for him to speak first. There was no way in hell she was going to risk upsetting the delicate social rules that separated them.

"Hello, Sara." Nikolai's deep voice had a raspy edge to it.

"Hello, Mr. Kalasnikov."

His brow arched at her ultra-respectful address. If he was impressed or pleased, he didn't say. Instead, he gestured to his wife and asked, "Have you met my wife, Vivian?"

Sara understood this was Nikolai's way of clearing the air and letting bygones be bygones. Besian and Ivan and Alexei would go back to Houston and tell people that Nikolai had introduced his wife to Sara, elevating her to a woman with acceptable status in the city. It was a very old school pardon.

"No, we haven't met." Sara held out her hand. "It's nice to meet you, Vivian."

"I feel like I kind of know you," Vivian said with a sweet smile. "I see your billboards and your ads all the time. We have a friend in common actually. That series that was shot for your fall campaign? The one with the sort of gothic feel to it? Niels did those, right?"

"Yes, he did. How do you know Niels?"

"Yuri," Vivian said. "Niels has done some photographs for me recently."

Sara didn't miss the tiniest twitch to Nikolai's jaw. Apparently the boss wasn't too pleased about his wife having photographs taken by Niels. Knowing what she did of Niels's style, especially his preference for shooting nudes or almost nudes, she didn't have to question why. "I'd love to see them sometime."

"The next time you're in Houston, you should come by the house. I'll show you the photographs Niels took for me. Maybe you'll even sit for me?"

Vivian's talent as an artist was well known to Sara. The thought of being her muse for a day was amusing. Sara glanced at Nikolai to see what he thought about that. He nodded stiffly as if to give his permission. "I'd love that, Vivian. Thank you."

After another minute or so of chitchat, Nikolai guided Vivian to Erin and Ivan. Besian quickly stepped over and said,

"That went better than I had expected."

Exhaling a relieved breath, Sara agreed with him. "Yes, it did."

Zel rubbed her lower back in a comforting way. If anyone could understand what it was like to live under the shadow of a powerful man, he could. In just under twenty-four hours, he would finally be set free from the chains binding him to the Beciraj crime family—if he won.

"Zel, if you need to duck out now and head back to your room to rest, I'll understand." Sara placed her hand on his chest and gazed up at him. "I want you to be in the best shape possible for tomorrow night."

He covered her hand with his. "Ivan has given me permission to stay for dinner. I have to rehydrate and refuel anyway. No alcohol or cake for me. Just lots of water and protein and carbohydrates."

She placed a flirtatious kiss on his jaw. "Don't worry. I'll drink enough champagne for both of us."

Zel dared to give her bottom a pat and kissed her forehead before taking her hand and guiding her toward the group now leaving the chapel for the private reception at the hotel's finest restaurant. Sara wasn't at all surprised that Alexei had managed to secure one of the best dining experiences in town for his wedding reception on such short notice. She didn't even want to imagine what it had cost to put all of this together for Shay.

As expected, the dinner party was fabulous. The wedding planners kept on staff by the Bellagio had outdone themselves for Alexei and Shay. Not a single detail had been overlooked. The luxurious setting seemed somehow intimate. The flesh flowers were amazing. Alcohol and food were in plentiful supply, all of it top shelf or Michelin star quality. The room buzzed with laughter and smiles. It was a beautiful night, and Sara was so happy she could share it with Alexei and his new wife—and Zel.

They sat side-by-side at a cozy little table near the bride and groom. Zel's hand was never far from her body. He seemed intent on maintaining a connection with her. She craved his body heat and snuggled in a bit closer to breathe in his incredible scent. The dinner served as extended foreplay for the pair, and by the time Alexei and Shay cut their cake, Sara was flushed and aching.

As if reading her mind, Zel tugged on her hand and dragged her away from the applauding crowd surround the newlyweds. She didn't fight him. Stomach fluttering, she happily followed him out of the restaurant. They made their way back to her suite, stopping in dark corners and hidden alcoves to make out like teenagers.

Something about the wedding had ignited a shared lust and need between them. Sara wanted Zel. Like right now. Tomorrow night she would be dancing another private show. He would be pounding the crap out of some other fighter. They were running out of time together.

Would tonight be their last night together?

Was it better that way? To end things with the fireworks of frantic lovemaking and then go their separate ways?

Zel was just the sort of guy she'd always imagined falling in love with. Smart, funny, handsome as hell and driven for success…

Getting involved with Zel would be only too easy but it

would just never work. He was obviously at a point in his life where he wanted stability, but she doubted she could provide that for him, not now. Her career required lots of traveling, incredibly late nights and hours of rehearsal. She didn't even have her own home at the moment, just a messy room in her mother's home and a mailbox at the business for all correspondence.

And, of course, the nightmare with Lalo's estate was just beginning. She fully expected to be recalled to Texas to deal with the DEA, ATF, FBI and the rest of the alphabet soup of federal agencies that would want to dig through her late husband's financial affairs. The legal bills would be incredible, and the stress would be unbearable. Zel didn't need any part of that. He was so close to escaping his underworld ties. She didn't need to drag him back to the dark side with her.

Recognizing that fact said something of her self-awareness, she supposed, but it didn't make it any easier. There was just something about Zel, something about their connection, that made her wonder if maybe, just maybe…

But it wouldn't do to dwell on the impossible. For the most part, Sara kept her feet firmly planted in reality, and in this reality, she simply couldn't be there for anyone right now. Zel deserved better than some half-assed attempt at a relationship.

When they reached the double doors of the suite, all of her worries and doubts fled. She was thinking about right now, this moment, with this wonderful man. Lust blossomed in her core. Nearly breathless with desire, Sara gripped Zel's hand as he unlocked the door and dragged her inside. He kicked the door shut behind them.

Watching the way he moved with predatory grace, she felt a thrill of excitement. His rough hands cupped her face as his mouth lowered to claim hers. She melted into him, whimpering softly against his searching tongue. But when he swept her off her feet and into his arms, Sara squealed in shock. "Ohmigod! Put me down before you break your back!"

He threw back his head and barked with laughter. "You're not that heavy."

Her eyes widened at his casual dismissal. She was, actually, quite heavy, but he wasn't the type for empty flattery. The way he effortlessly carted her through the suite convinced her he wasn't just acting macho. She really wasn't that heavy—to him, at least.

When they reached the dining area, he knocked aside a chair and placed her on the table. Very hastily, he shrugged out of his suit jacket. Eyes wild with lust, Zel dropped to his knees and grasped the hem of her dress. He shoved it up around her waist and yanked on her thong, jerking it down her thighs and calves and over her ankle.

As he pushed her thighs wide open, Sara shuddered. The brush of air against her naked sex felt cool. She arched off the table as Zel's pointed tongue swiped her slit and flicked her clit. The delicious sensation of his lapping tongue drove her insane.

Clutching at the table, Sara bucked against his mouth. His stiffened tongue dipped inside her and fluttered over her clitoris. Overwhelmed, she shrieked and clasped his head, keeping him *right* there. It just felt so fucking good. She was going to burst any second. Zel overpowered her clasp and worked his tongue around her clit. He sucked the bud between his lips, heightening the sensation.

Thighs clenching, stomach tightening, Sara breathed erratically as her orgasm built. Stunned by the power of the explosion, she gasped and undulated wildly atop the table. Toes curling, she slapped the tabletop. Her mouth hung open, only unintelligible *ahs* and moans escaping. Zel kept torturing her until she put her foot against his shoulder and gently shoved him away. "Enough," she panted. "Enough."

He nuzzled her inner thigh and teasingly bit the plump flesh there. She giggled at the ticklish sensation. Slowly, he rose to his feet and peeled off his button-down shirt and dropped it to the floor where it joined his jacket. He took a condom from his wallet, and Sara licked her lips. She ached to be stretched and filled by him again.

Pants lowered, Zel moved between her legs, his condom-covered cock standing fully erect. He grasped his dick in his hand and traced her labia with it, rubbing it in circles around her still-sensitive clit. The sharp sensation made her jump a bit. Lined up with her body, Zel plunged into her wet depths. He leaned over and caught her mouth in a searing kiss.

As he took her with long, deep strokes, Sara ran her hands down his back, loving every inch of the muscles rippling beneath her fingers. With that incredible physique, he exemplified masculinity at its finest. The flexing sinews made her feel like some fragile flower in need of protection and the most delicate of touches. No other lover had ever affected her in this way, and Sara found it most intoxicating.

Zel shifted into a standing position. The new angle of his cock took her breath away. He grabbed her hand and sucked her fingers between his lips. Her belly quivered as his velvety tongue suckled her fingertips. When he placed her fingers against her clit, she understood his silent message. Sara rubbed her slick nub and clenched her pussy around his thrusting cock. He grasped her thighs for leverage, his fingers biting into her skin as he pounded into her. Sara slid up and down the tabletop, her dress bunching around her waist.

Trembling with need, Sara concentrated on the coiling sensation in her lower belly. Her heels pressed into Zel's ass as she urged him to fuck her harder, faster. Fingers moving quickly, Sara bit her lower lip as the first faint flutters of an orgasm rocked her core. Zel's thrusts reached a breakneck pace as he now sought his release. The sound of their bodies slapping together filled the room. Sara whispered his name again and again as she continued massaging her pulsing clit to draw out every last bit of sensation from her orgasm.

Zel slammed into her so hard she gasped. Eyes clamped tightly, he shuddered and jerked as he came. Sara clutched at his abs, her fingernails lightly scratching his bronzed torso. She had a sudden desperate need to kiss him, to feel his lips on hers. As if sensing her need, Zel bent down and kissed her so sweetly, his hand lovingly caressing her face. When he pulled back, the tenderness in his gaze nearly brought tears to her eyes. Sara blinked hard against the prickling sensation, refusing to show just how much she actually cared about him.

He planted a playful kiss on the tip of her nose before standing and pulling out of her. Sara whimpered at the sudden loss of him between her thighs. Smiling, Zel grasped her hands and hauled her into a sitting position. His fingers tangled in her hair as he brought their mouths together again. Worried this might be one of their last kisses, Sara made it count, cupping his square jaw and caressing his face. She wanted to memorize every last detail.

A knock at the door interrupted their lingering, sweet moment. They both eyed the doors with irritated glances. Sighing, Sara said, "It's probably bell service. Lucy took a private car to the airport to pick up her wife. They were going right out to a show and dinner. It's probably Molly's luggage."

He kissed her tenderly. "I'll take care of it."

"I'm going to tidy up." She carefully slipped off the table and tugged her skirt back down until it covered her thighs. Zel zipped his pants and pocketed her discarded thong before slipping back into his shirt. He didn't bother to button it.

Carefree and comfortable in his skin, he strode toward the door while she scurried into the master suite. She had just ducked into the bathroom when she heard Zel raise his voice in anger. "What the fuck are you doing here?"

"I guess I'm here to kick your ass!"

A moment later, the unmistakable sounds of a scuffle filled the penthouse. She rushed back into the living area of the penthouse just in time to see Zel and Ramsay tumble across the floor. Stunned, Sara gaped at the mayhem and violence before her.

What is he doing here?

Ramsay kicked out his leg, knocking over a coffee table, as Zel took him down to the marble floor. The glass tabletop shattered when it whacked the floor. The shards sprayed everywhere. A large piece sliced into Ramsay, cutting his back or his arm. He was moving so much that Sara couldn't tell where, exactly, he had been injured.

Desperate to keep Zel from getting hurt, she stepped forward to intervene. Zel must have seen her because he snarled, "Don't!"

Ramsay took advantage of Zel's moment of inattention to strike. He snatched up a huge piece of glass and jabbed it close to Zel's throat. Sara gasped as Zel went to the floor, knocked onto his back as Ramsay threatened to slit his throat.

And then she saw it.

A gun.

Right there.

On the floor.

Without thinking, she picked it up and pointed it right at Ramsay's face. Wondering if she could hit a target so small, she lowered it to his broad chest. "You put that glass down right now, or I'll shoot."

Ramsay laughed. "No, you won't."

"I will!"

"You'll miss," Ramsay retorted, clearly unworried that a gun—his gun—was being pointed right at him.

"She might," a familiar voice said from behind her, "but I won't..."

CHAPTER SEVEN

SARA GLANCED AT the open doorway of the penthouse where Besian had appeared like some twisted version of a guardian angel. Weapon in hand, he kept it pointed steadily at Ramsay's head as he closed the door to the suite and advanced into the room. "I feel lucky tonight. Let's put odds on it, Ramsay. What do you say?"

Gulping hard, Ramsay seemed to realize he was caught. He moved the glass away from Zel's neck. A thin stream of blood rolled down Zel's neck and onto the floor. In the next breath, Zel showed his physical prowess by shoving off the floor, arching up onto his shoulders, and flipping Ramsay onto his back. Zel got the upper hand, wrapping his legs around Ramsay's waist and clamping her stepbrother's head between his meaty forearms. Ramsay tried to get free but it was no use. His heavy body began to sag until he passed out cold.

The sounds of Zel's heavy breathing filled the room. Blood pooled around Ramsay's body. Panicked, she lowered the gun and asked, "Is he dead?"

Zel touched Ramsay's neck as if to search for a pulse. "He's alive."

"Get away from him," Besian ordered, flicking the safety onto his own weapon and holstering it. Stepping up close, he said, "Sara, give me the gun."

She held still as Besian gingerly removed the weapon, emptied the chamber and the magazine, and rendered it safe. Still shocked by his unexpected appearance, she asked, "What are you doing here?"

"You disappeared from the reception. I figured you and Zel had come back here to play. I knew that Ivan wanted him in bed early so I thought I would come up here and see if you wanted to go gamble with me. Like old times," he said with a reminiscent smile that faded as his gaze landed on Ramsay. "I guess this really *is* like old times."

"I'm so sorry," she said on a rushed breath. "I didn't know he would go this far."

"He's a crazy bastard," Besian grumbled. Walking to Zel and Ramsay, he crouched down and touched Zel's neck. "It's a bleeder but you're not going to need stitches. It will be impossible to hide tomorrow."

"I cut myself shaving." Zel practiced his lie, and Sara hated herself for putting him in this position.

"Help me." Besian motioned toward the heavier man's body. Together, they rolled Ramsay onto his side and found the gash on the back of his arm. "Sara, get some towels."

"Put on some shoes," Zel added. "There's glass everywhere."

She did as instructed, finding her slippers and towels and rushing back to the men. They tightly wound a towel around the nasty gash on Ramsay's arm to stem the blood flow. There were smaller gashes and cuts on the back of his head and up and down his back. He wasn't going to bleed to death, but he would need stitches when he woke up.

Sara sat back on her heels and looked at the mess surrounding them. Broken glass. A passed out and bleeding ex-con. Zel's face was bloody, and he was awkwardly holding his left hand. *Oh, no...*

"Your hand? Is it—?"

"It's fine." Zel's answer came clipped and harsh as he stretched out his fingers. He moved carefully, and she worried that he had broken something.

Judging by the look on Besian's face, he thought the same thing. Sighing, the boss said, "We need to get Ramsay out of here."

"Without anyone seeing him? Without security being called?" Sara rubbed her face between her hands. "If he makes a scene, they'll drag us all down to the police station. What will happen to Zel's fight?"

Zel's jaw visibly tightened. He had to be thinking the same thing she was. The scandal would ruin him. One dogged journalist with the right sources could find out everything about Zel's history and hers and blow up their secrets. The fallout would put their lives in danger. Besian was their connection to the Albanian mafia, and he had shielded them for years. But Luka, his boss—his blood—back in Tirana would end them in a heartbeat to protect the Beciraj family.

"Zel, get dressed and go back to your room." Besian was already pulling out his cell phone and making a call. "I'm sending Ivan to meet you."

"I'm not leaving Sara."

Besian's gaze darkened in that terrifying way he had perfected. It was that stare he used to remind grown men like Zel that he could make them disappear with a snap of his fingers.

"I wasn't asking."

Zel wasn't going to back down. Still amped up from his fight, he stepped forward, and Sara reacted instantly. The instinct to protect Zel was so strong. She moved between both men and put her hand on Zel's chest in a soothing gesture. Gazing up at him, she pleaded, "Please go."

Seemingly taken aback, Zel asked, "You want *me* to leave? You want *him* to stay?"

Sara swallowed anxiously. "I trust him."

"More than me?"

In that moment, Sara understood what had to be done. Zel was the finest man she had ever known. He was good inside. He was the kind of man who was going to make some woman very happy someday. He would be a wonderful husband and a father—just never with her.

Because you're poison.

It was a memory from long ago that resurfaced. Lalo's voice filled her head as he hissed his venom at her. Some part of her had always believed him. Every single relationship she'd had with a man had ended badly. Maybe Lalo had been right. Maybe there was something wrong with her.

"I don't know you, Zel," she said finally. "I've known Besian for ten years."

"I see," he ground out the words between gritted teeth.

He didn't see, and she was glad. She was relieved he couldn't see the way she was breaking apart inside as she hurt him so cruelly.

As if unable to walk away without fighting for her, he touched her face. "Sara, I think we have something real between us. We'd be stupid to let a chance like this go."

"You would be stupid to stay with me." She stepped away from him, away from the warm hand touching her so gently, and gestured to the door. "You need to leave now."

Pain flashed across his face. She felt sick for having hurt him.

"I'll go," he said finally. Clearly upset, he strode to the door without as much as a sideways glance in her direction. Zel yanked open the door, and Sara realized she couldn't let him leave like this.

"Zel, wait!"

He stopped abruptly. Slowly he pivoted to face her. His steeled expression made her wince. "What?"

She gulped under his angry glare. "I'm sorry."

His cheek twitched. "I don't think you are."

Hot tears stung her eyes. "I didn't mean for it to end like this."

"No one ever does."

His piece said, Zel left, slamming the door behind him. Sara stared at the door for a long time, until Besian finally put a cautious hand on her shoulder. With a friendly squeeze, he said, "Sara, go into the bedroom and close the door. I'll come get you when it's safe."

Numb and cold, she glanced around the destroyed living room. She suddenly remembered something very important. "Lucy and Molly are here. They're doing dinner and a show and then some gambling."

"I'll take care of it, Sara. They'll never know this happened."

She didn't dare ask him for the details. Besian's connections weren't limited to Houston. He'd built his empire back home on loans and gambling. He spent a lot of time in Vegas and knew all the right people here. Like a stage magician, he would wave his hand and make this whole mess disappear.

Her gaze lingered on Ramsay who seemed to be coming around. He had come here with malicious intent tonight yet she couldn't condemn him. Touching Besian's arm, she said, "Please don't kill him."

"He came all the way from Houston to harass you, Sara. He brought a gun to your door. If Zel hadn't been here, Ramsay would have kidnapped or killed you."

"He didn't hurt me. He's a terrible person," she agreed, "but I don't think either one of us needs his death on our consciences."

"If he won't cooperate?" Besian slashed his hand in front of his throat. "He's done."

Mutely, she nodded. Besian pointed to the bedroom, and she picked up the clutch she had discarded earlier and retreated to the safety of the master suite. She checked her phone and expelled a relieved breath when she saw Lucy's messages. Her sister and sister-in-law had decided to make a wild night of it and didn't think they would be back to the room until the very, very early hours of the morning.

Not wanting to hear anything that was happening in the living room of the penthouse, Sara turned on the television and then made her way into the bathroom for a long, hot shower. When she sat on the tiled bench, she broke down, burying her face in her hands and sobbing as the warm water spilled over her tired body.

Just a few hours ago, she had been sitting next to Zel, watching Shay and Alexei get married while dreaming of all the possibilities a future with him presented. Now? Now she was shattered inside, broken like a mirror. In her mind, she tabulated the many mistakes she had made in her life. There were so many decisions she questioned, so many things she regretted.

If only. If only. If only.

But this was the real world, and in the real world, she had to live with her choices and her mistakes. If that meant that she had to live her life alone? Well…so be it.

"Sara?" Besian knocked on the bathroom door. "Are you all right?"

Clearing her throat, she wiped at her eyes. "I'll be out in a few minutes."

Heartsick and broken, she finished her shower and changed into a pair of comfortable pajama bottoms and an old t-shirt. She found Besian kicked back on the couch in the master suite, a glass of scotch in one hand while he rubbed the back of his neck with the other. He seemed tired, more tired than usual, and leaner. It had only been a handful of months since he'd been shot. He'd returned to work remarkably fast, maybe even too fast.

"Stop looking at me like that," he grumbled. "I'm not an invalid."

"I didn't say you were."

"You didn't have to," he groused. He gestured to the room service spread of late night snacks and alcohol. Holding up a glass of white wine, he said, "It's your favorite."

Moscato. Of course. She dropped onto the cushion next to Besian and took a long, deep drink of the sweet wine.

Besian's eyebrows shot toward his hairline. "I guess it's a

good thing I ordered a whole bottle."

"Yep," she said, already sitting forward to refill her glass. "I'm not going to ask about Ramsay."

"I wouldn't suggest it," he dryly replied. "It's done. He's gone. You won't have to worry about him ever again."

She didn't ask about the security tapes that were sure to have his face on them. Besian he had probably paid to make them disappear, or he'd used a local cleaner to tidy up the loose ends.

"Housekeeping cleaned away all the glass and blood. The concierge will send up a new table tomorrow. It's going on my bill. I told him that I had a little too much to drink and tripped."

"You should have blamed it on me."

He shrugged. "They know me here."

"You haven't partied like that in years."

"That's what happens when you get old like me," he warned with a playful smile.

She rolled her eyes. "You're not old."

"I feel old." He rubbed his chest again.

"You were shot. You're supposed to hurt and feel old after that."

"It's more than that," he said, his voice wistful and his gaze dark. "I was sitting there watching Alexei marry Shay, and it hit me. I'm the last one who isn't dead or married. Ivan? Married. Alexei? Married. Nikolai? Married. Julio? Dead. Lorenzo? Dead. Lalo? Dead." He shook his head. "This life tried to kill me—and nearly succeeded."

"But you're alive," she insisted.

"For what? To make money? What the fuck kind of life is

that? I have power. I have money. I have a beautiful home, cars, property…"

"But you're alone," she finished for him.

He nodded. "I'm alone."

"You don't have to be alone, Besian. You're surrounded by women all day long—"

"I don't want a dancer."

She popped his arm. "Hey!"

"That's *not* what I meant and you know it." He took a long drink of his scotch. "I respect the girls who dance for me. I've even dated some of them."

"But mixing business and pleasure doesn't work?"

"It does for some men. It might have worked for me, but then I saw her and—"

"Oh my God!" she reacted with shock as she finally understood what he was trying to say. "Who is she?"

He wouldn't meet her searching gaze. "It's complicated."

"It always is, Besian."

He drained the last of his glass. "She's too good for me. If she's smart, she'll stay far away and forget I even exist."

Sara started to protest, but then she considered what she had just done with Zel. She had sent him away to protect him, feeling the same way that Besian did about this unknown woman who had stolen his heart.

Dropping back against the couch, Besian said, "You know why Ramsay was here." It wasn't a question. "He made the reasons for his visit clear to me when I gave him his options."

"He thinks I owe him money."

"You *do* owe him money."

She glared at Besian. "How the hell do you figure that?"

"He went to *la pinta* thinking his boss had his back, and he comes out and Lalo fucked him." Besian made a crude gesture. "Then, to get Ramsay to stop causing problems, he had the bastard framed and sent back to prison. Yes, your stepbrother is an asshole, but he's not wrong about Lalo and the money. You just inherited everything Lalo owned and that includes his debts. So, technically, according to the rules of our underworld, *you* do owe him."

"And how do you propose I pay him? Huh? I can't touch the assets that Lalo put in my name. I'll be the one who ends up in *la pinta*!" She shook her head. "I don't want any of it. Not a penny."

"That's good because the government is probably going to take all of it, even the shit you bought with your own money."

"Good. I want that part of my life closed. I want it to be over. Finished." She spread her hands out in front of her, only narrowly avoiding sloshing wine. "I want to be able to come back to Houston and not have to look over my shoulder every five seconds."

"You'll be safe in Houston. Nikolai's blessing earlier made sure of that."

"I'll need a good lawyer to handle the inheritance bullshit."

"I know someone you can trust. He's on Nikolai's payroll." Besian touched his wrist as if to make a point that the lawyer was part of the family. "As far as Ramsay is concerned, I've taken care of it. He'll get what he thinks he's owed when he's resettled." He made a dismissive gesture. "We'll work out the specifics of repayment later."

"So that's that," she said quietly, already feeling herself drawn back into the Albanian mafia's stranglehold.

"Not like that," Besian countered. "This is a personal debt. It's private between you and me. I promised you that once you paid your debts, you would be free of the family. I'm keeping that promise. This is a friend helping a friend."

As Sara thought about how much Besian had risked to keep her safe in the many years they had been friends, her gaze drifted to the television still playing across the bedroom. She zeroed in on images of Zel. After seeing him fight in the flesh on the penthouse floor, it was a different thing altogether to see him fighting on television. The cherry-picked images and reels showed him at his very best, pummeling and twisting and kicking and subduing his opponents.

But then the voice-over switched to a harrowing recall of Zel's opponent's history. Mace was a hard-faced, snub-nosed brawler. Almost all of Mace's highlight reels featured blood spatter and unconscious opponents. The stats shown made little sense to Sara, but the clips of Mace striking an opponent so hard he dropped like a bag of rocks made her chest constrict.

Learning Mace had killed the man made her very nearly ill.

Swallowing hard as her stomach roiled with nausea, Sara looked at Besian. "Zel is fighting *that* man?"

Besian nodded. "He's the toughest opponent Zel's ever faced. Actually, Zel did the league a favor by stepping in to cover this fight when the originally scheduled fighter went down with a bad injury."

"Mace killed a man!"

"Not on purpose."

"Like that makes it any better?" Sara shook her head. "He

can't go through with this, Besian."

Besian seemed amused by her sudden concern. "This is what he does, Sara. It's the risk he takes."

"It's stupid! He's risking his life for what? Some money?"

Besian held her gaze. "Zel is risking his life for his freedom."

"How much?" It was a dangerous question to ask, but she did it anyway.

"Sara…"

"Besian."

"It's a lot. More than you can risk."

"What are the odds?"

Besian hesitated. "Mace is at -300. Zel is the dog at +340."

"Your book is still open?"

"Sara," he said with a warning sigh. "You don't want to take any of this action."

"I'm a big girl. I know what I'm doing."

"You're a *terrible* gambler. You always have been. I'm not taking your money."

"Then I'll go find someone else who will," she threatened.

"You know that our friendship won't protect you from the debt," he warned. "That money goes into the family pool. You make your payments on time—"

"Or you go after my kneecaps," she said with a roll of her eyes. "I've heard it before, Besian."

"I'm not taking your money tonight. Not when you've been drinking," he decided. "If you're still serious, come see me tomorrow. I'll put you in the book."

"When I win, I want you to apply my winnings to Zel's debt. Whatever is left over goes to him."

He snorted with something akin to amusement. "You would do something romantic like that."

"Zel and I can't be together, but that doesn't mean I can't help him."

"I don't think he wants your money, Sara."

"Trust me. He's better off with the money."

"If you say so…" Stretching out his legs, Besian exhaled roughly. "There's something you need to know about Lalo's death."

She swallowed nervously. "All right."

"I'm telling you this because I trust you and I think you need to know," he said carefully. "It involves Alexei and Shay." He eyed her almost empty glass. "You might want to refill before I start this story…"

CHAPTER EIGHT

TENSE AND IRRITATED, Ivan shut off the water and stepped out of the shower. He grabbed the towel draped over the nearby bar and wrapped it around his waist. He expected some tension and stress on the morning of a fight. He was always worried that he hadn't prepared his men for their contests.

Had he drilled them enough? Had they sparred enough? Had they improved their ground game? Had he worked them too hard? Pushed them to drop too much weight? He was always mentally cataloguing their injuries and weaknesses and comparing them to their opponents, always working the angles and looking for any last-minute advantage.

But this stress that was eating up his stomach and making his neck ache? This was all Zel and that bullshit with the dancing girl.

When Besian had called to tell him to meet Zel in his room, he hadn't known what to expect. Finding his fighter with a bloody neck and bruised hand had been something of a relief. He'd been expecting much, much worse. The hand wasn't broken, just banged up, and the cut could be explained away as a shaving accident. Zel would be able to fight tonight, but his heart and his head were out of the game. Men who weren't focused got hurt—and they got hurt badly. Sometimes they fucking died.

"You're going to have a stroke if you don't calm down," Erin warned, her voice gentle but firm. She leaned against the doorframe, her ankles crossed and her toes pointed like a ballerina as she watched him with a worried eye. A sheer pink lace and silk nightie barely covered her perfect ass. Always effortlessly beautiful, she was at her loveliest like this. Tousled hair. Sleepy eyes. No makeup. Just natural, pretty Erin.

"I'm going to have a stroke if you keep walking around in that tiny little thing," he retorted gruffly. Her bare bottom and her nipples were plainly visible in the see-through nightgown. "I hope you don't intend to answer the door like that when our breakfast gets here."

She rolled her eyes at his possessive remark. It was one of their games. He played up his caveman side, and she pretended not to like it. "Actually, I had planned to walk around naked this morning. I figured you would tear this off of me the second you saw it last night."

There was no mistaking her annoyed tone. After all that champagne and dancing, Erin had been hot for him last night. Hell, she'd ended up on his lap during the cab ride back to the hotel.

He'd been aching for her, already planning out all the ways he was going to make her scream his name, when his iPhone started rattling in his pocket. Instead of a passionate night with his wife, he'd spent hours in Zel's hotel room icing the fighter's bruised hand and watching that cut on his neck scab over while examining him for any signs of head trauma or invisible injuries that would end his fighting chances.

"Evie?"

He hadn't been fond of her nickname when she'd first started teasingly calling him Evie, twisting up the proper Russian pronunciation of his name to needle him during an argument one night. Somehow, that nickname had stuck and soon he found that he rather liked it. To everyone else he was Ivan or Vanya or Coach. For her and her alone, he answered to Evie.

Erin advanced on him with deliberate steps. She placed a small hand on his chest, her skin soft and cool against his. Rising on tiptoes, she kissed his jaw. "You're going to develop an ulcer if you keep worrying like this."

He slid his arms around her slim waist and nuzzled her cheek. "If I could snap my fingers and relax, I would."

"I know how to help you relax." She walked her fingers down the flat plane of his stomach and pressed ticklish kisses across his chest. His body reacted instantly to her teasing touch. He swallowed hard as Erin kissed her way down his stomach before gracefully kneeling at his feet. She cupped his stiffening cock through the damp fabric of the towel and nipped at his happy trail.

After she peeled away the towel, she grasped his cock, and he shivered with excitement and lust. She stroked him, dragging her hand up and down his shaft while gazing up at him with so much love. He didn't deserve this. He didn't deserve this innocent beauty who had chosen to love him despite the black stains in his history. When she smiled at him like that, he felt as if he could conquer the world. She made him feel invincible. She made him want to be her hero.

And—*fuck*—when she wrapped her wet lips around the head of his cock, she owned him. Anything she wanted, he would give. Anything. Diamonds? A new house? A new car? A trip to the Caribbean? A weekend in Paris? Hers. Done. Without question.

But she never asked.

She gave and she loved and she supported him without holding out her hand or running a tab. She was totally selfless when it came to her love for him—and he would spend the rest of his life working hard to deserve it.

With a mischievous grin, she flicked her tongue along the sensitive underside of his cock before sucking him deep and hard. He gripped the edge of the marble vanity behind him so tightly he was shocked it didn't snap. She hummed enthusiastically around his dick and took him even deeper. His heart slammed against his ribcage. She sucked and fluttered her tongue while stroking him.

During their earliest days together, he had experienced such guilt in moments like these. He had put her on a pedestal, elevating her above all women and denying himself the rougher pleasures he liked from fear of hurting or disgusting her. When she had finally asked him to play rough, to spank her a little harder, to tug her hair, to nip at her neck or breast, he had been floored. It had taken him a while to accept that she wanted everything he had to offer and that she enjoyed it just as much as he did.

So when she dragged his hand away from the counter and toward her hair, he knew exactly what she wanted. He threaded his fingers through her silky hair and gripped a handful of it, pulling just enough to sting but never enough to harm. She smiled excitedly around his cock before relaxing her jaw. He thrust into her mouth. It felt so fucking good. He wouldn't last long.

When Erin reached between her legs to touch herself, he lost control. He groaned her name before the first burst of his orgasm punched the air right out of his lungs. Erin moaned enthusiastically and took him deep into her mouth, greedily swallowing his seed. When she'd milked him dry, she left him shuddering by gently sucking and licking his sensitive cock until he was soft and slipped from her mouth.

Looking thoroughly pleased with herself, Erin sat back on her heels and licked her lips. She reminded him of a naughty kitten, and he couldn't help but smile down at her. He helped her stand and then dragged her tight to his body for a kiss that left her breathless and shaking. His hand traveled the curve of her spine to her bare bottom. He squeezed a handful of her plump ass before giving her a sound smack that made her press even harder against him.

As if on cue, there was a knock at the door of their suite. He traced his thumb along her lower lip and held her smoky gaze. "Fuck those pancakes. I'm going to have you for breakfast instead."

"I don't know. I think I'd rather have my mimosa and English muffin instead." With a daring smile, she crept away from him and out of the bathroom. Knowing his wife as well as he did, he understood this was a bit of teasing and foreplay. She would go all the way to that door in nothing but that see-through nightgown.

All right, he thought with a surge of desire. *Challenge accepted.*

In seven quick, powerful strides, he caught up with his wife and swung her up into his arms. She squealed with laughter, giggling even louder when he buried his face along the curve of her neck and nipped at her throat. He carried her to the bed and dropped her onto it. She tried to sit up, but he pushed her back down, using his big hand to gently hold her in place. Her breaths quickened as he opened her thighs and bared her pussy to his approving gaze.

There was another knock at the door as he lowered his face and kissed her right there, brushing his lips against her soft pink heat. Holding her gaze, he said, "You stay right here." He dragged his mouth down her slit. "Just like this."

She gulped and nodded shakily. "I won't move."

He rose to his full height and snatched up the pair of pajama bottoms he had shucked earlier. After slipping into them, he headed left the bedroom. He made sure the door was open just a few inches, enough for Erin to worry that another man might see her in that exposed and vulnerable position. Ivan would never let that happen, but he liked the idea of teasing her with the possibility.

The hotel porter's eyes widened at the sight of all his tattoos, but the young kid seemed to know better than to stare or ask stupid questions. The porter quickly uncovered the dishes to make sure everything was there and handed over the room service ticket. Ivan added a tip, signed the bottom and handed it back. He practically chased the kid out of the suite and locked the door behind him.

Back in the bedroom, he pounced on Erin. She laughed at his enthusiasm and then moaned as his tongue did wicked things to her. He forced her thighs wide open, holding her right where he wanted her, and went wild on her pussy. She was soaking wet for him.

Giving head excited her so much that he always had an easy time of giving her pleasure when it was her turn. This morning was no exception. She arched her back and rocked her hips as he fluttered his tongue over her in the way she loved best.

"Evie," she breathed his name. The muscles in her legs flexed, and she began to inhale deeper, faster breaths. "Evie!"

She came hard while shouting his name. His ego enjoyed the exaltation, and he made sure not to let up until she was inching away from his mouth and gasping from the after-shocks. He spent a little time licking and nibbling her pussy and clit until she sagged, boneless and spent, atop the messy bed. He trailed his mouth along her inner thigh and across her belly, pushing the see-through nightie out of the way as he crawled up her body.

Eye to eye, they smiled at one another, sharing the inti-mate looks that married couples did. Mornings like this, he couldn't quite believe he shared his life with this incredible woman. She cupped his face in her hands and caressed his cheek with her thumbs. She seemed so fragile to him, her fingers so elegant and fine. He felt like a brute next to her, all muscle and brawn and rough edges.

"What are you thinking about?" she asked softly. "You look so serious."

"I'm wondering what the hell you see in me and my horri-ble face."

"Your face is not horrible! You're handsome." She kissed him lovingly. "You're the sexiest man in the world to me."

"*Angil moy.*" He laughed and kissed her back. "My face is like an old potato."

She scoffed and traced the dip in his nose where it had been broken twice. "I love your old potato face." She ran her finger along the dent in his forehead and the scar on his cheek. "I love everything about you, Ivan. These scars, these old wounds, your tattoos—you're perfect to me."

No matter how many times she professed her love, he couldn't eradicate the fear that someday she would wake up and realize she could have done so much better. He had talked to Dimitri about it once, after too many beers, and Dimitri had helped him understand that being abandoned as a child had left a dark, ugly hole inside him. Erin's love had poured into that hole, but he feared it would never be completely filled.

As if reading his mind, she embraced him and kissed his cheek. "I love you so much."

Closing his eyes, he hugged her back and kissed her forehead. "I love you, Erin."

When he dropped onto his back next to her, Erin snuggled up close. She traced the inked lines on his chest. "I don't say it enough, but I'm so proud of you. I'm so proud of everything you've built."

"I don't know what I would do without you," he admitted, turning his head so she could see the sincere look on his face. "Everything I've built since we got together? That's all you, Erin. That's you pushing me and forcing me to see the warehouse as something bigger than just a local gym."

"That warehouse is your future," she insisted. "It's your legacy."

"*Our* legacy," he corrected. "It's ours."

She touched his jaw. "Is that why you're so stressed out today? Are you worried that we'll have a setback if Zel loses tonight?"

He expelled a troubled breath. "If he loses, we'll be fine. We have two other fighters showcased tonight. Kir will win in the first round," he said with certainty. "TKO," he added. "You know what he's like once he steps in the ring."

She nodded. "He's a beast."

"And Javi will be walking out of his fight tonight one step closer to the featherweight title match," he continued, thinking of the former Hermanos gang member who had wandered into his gym two years ago with big dreams and an explosive kick. "We're going to have a strong showing tonight."

"Even if Zel takes a loss?"

"The possibility of Zel losing isn't my main concern. If he loses? He loses. It happens. No." He sighed. "I'm worried he'll get hurt. *Bad*," he added. "Zel's head is all fucked up. He's so torn up about Sara he's not thinking straight. Mace is dangerous. That man can *hit*. He's like Sergei. That punch? It's deadly. If Zel isn't right up here," he tapped his skull, "he might not block and defend."

Erin lifted up on her elbow and rested her head in the palm of her hand. She studied him carefully. "Are you going to pull him from the fight?"

Ivan met his wife's questioning gaze. "No." He had made that decision and would stick with it. "Physically, he's fine. He's not anymore banged up than any other fighter that steps into the ring on fight night. They all come to their matches with bruises and mild injuries. It's part of the life. He says he can get his head right before tonight."

"Do you believe him?"

He didn't answer immediately. "I trust him to know if he's

ready."

"He's been through so much," she said quietly. "He's lost so much. He might not be thinking clearly, Ivan."

He wiped a hand down his face. She was right, of course. "I told him to stay away from Sara, but I let him guilt me into cutting him some slack. I feel sick thinking about the way I encouraged him to be with her. I knew better!" he exclaimed angrily. "I fucking knew better. That woman is like poison."

"Why would you say that?" Erin sounded upset. "She's a lovely person. I enjoyed her company last night."

"One night isn't enough to get to know someone."

"Oh really?"

He knew exactly what she meant, and he didn't care for the comparison. "That's different, Erin. *You* were different."

"Why? How? Because I'm not a dancer?"

"No." Turning on his side so he could maintain eye contact, he said, "You were innocent when you came into my gym for help. You didn't steal. You didn't deal drugs. You lived a good, clean life. You were just trying to save your sister."

"Unless there's something else about Sara you haven't told me, the only mistake she made was falling in love with the wrong man. She was young. It happens. She shouldn't be punished for that for the rest of her life."

He grunted roughly, not wanting to admit that his wife was right.

Erin interlaced their hands. She brushed her lips against his temple and cheek. "Listen, I nearly got you killed. I brought a mess to your doorstep, but that didn't stop you from helping me. Everyone warned you. They told you to stay away and to be smart. Did you listen?"

He sent a mock annoyed glance her way. "I'm beginning to think I should have."

She playfully bit his earlobe. "Hush! You know that you'd be miserable without me."

"I would," he agreed. "There's no argument there."

She kissed him, her lips lingering on his. "Ivan, you protected me. You took care of me. You loved me." She squeezed his hand. "What's wrong with Zel doing the same thing for Sara?"

"I don't know," he grumbled.

"What if she's the one, Ivan? What if he feels the same way about Sara that I felt about you?"

He perked to that. "How did you feel about me?"

She actually blushed. "You were so wrong for me, but when I walked out of your office, I knew you were the man that was going to change my life."

"I knew that I was going to marry you by the end of that first night," he admitted. "I felt it here." He touched his chest. "I'd never felt that until you."

"What if that's the way Zel feels about Sara?"

Ivan sighed. "Then I suppose you're going to cook up some plan to get them back together."

"I'm already on it," she confessed with an impish smile. "I texted Besian first thing this morning. We're working out the details now."

His eyes widened with concern. "Erin, I don't want you text messaging Besian. Have you forgotten that he wanted to hurt you?"

"I haven't forgotten. It was a long time ago. It was different circumstances. I've forgiven him and moved on from that night."

"Not that long ago!" Ivan scoffed. "And how the hell did you get his number? Has he been bothering you?"

"I got it from Vivian. She—"

"—is trouble!" he cut in sharply. "I can't wait to tell Kolya that his wife is hooking my wife up with a loan shark."

Erin rolled her eyes. "Are you done acting ridiculous?"

"No."

"Fine." She surprised him by pushing off the mattress and sliding her leg across his hip. Straddling his lap, she grasped the bottom of her little nightie and dragged it up and over her head. Naked and wanting him, she planted both hands on his chest and leaned down to kiss him. "I guess I have no choice but to distract you and make you forget all about my scheming."

"Erin," he said, his voice rough with need as she stroked his cock back to hardness. "If we keep this up, you'll have a belly as big as Vivian's by summer."

Laughing, she sat up and wiggled her backside until she had him right where she wanted him. She bit her lower lip as she sank down on his rock hard shaft. "I'm counting on it…"

CHAPTER NINE

B LACK HAIR WHIPPING wildly, Sara shook what her mama gave her center stage at Vegas' hottest punk club. Queen's *Fat Bottomed Girls* blared over the sound system as she performed her brand-new number for the thirtieth birthday bash of BJ Barnes, the lead singer of the infamous punk rock band Blue Sunday.

Dressed like a sassy fifties pinup, Sara worked the crowd into a frenzy as she teased them with the slow removal of her polka dot dress. The sight of her plump curves in vintage cherry red lingerie set them off. She smoothed her hands over the swell of her breasts and along the satin shaper hugging her tummy and hips. Tipped forward in her red heels, Sara sashayed to the antique convertible parked stage left and crawled onto the hood. Her catlike movements showed off her best assets and had the crowd catcalling.

With the grace of a gymnast, Sara carefully balanced on the hood, her heels finding traction on the safety mat her crew had put in place. Rocking side to side, she unhooked the back of the shaper and peeled it away from her body. She tossed it overhead and did a sexy spin atop the hood, giving everyone a good look at the lacy briefs covering her voluptuous ass. Sara gave her backside a hearty smack.

The roar of approval sent shivers down her spine. Tonight, more than ever, Sara desperately needed the energy of the pumped-up crowd. Despite being utterly heartbroken, she approached this engagement with the utmost professionalism. BJ deserved to feel like the center of her attention. Feeding off the crowd allowed Sara to play up her sexiness and mischievous nature.

Hips swiveling, she crouched low and gave them a peek between her thighs before sitting down on the edge of the hood. Her legs dangled over the side as she kicked off her pumps and then made a show of unsnapping her garters and peeling off one black stocking and then the other. She used one stocking as a prop, holding it beneath her breasts as she gave them a wild shake.

Legs bare, Sara dropped the stocking and slid off the hood. She danced back to center stage and hooked her thumbs in the lacy red briefs. Undulating like a belly dancer, Sara dragged the panties down her ample hips inch by teasing inch to reveal a red G-string and the words "Happy Birthday BJ" emblazoned across her ass cheeks in fiery orange paint. The whistles and clapping nearly drowned out the music.

She stepped out of her panties and strutted downstage until she could almost touch the crowd. Sara made quick work of dispensing her bra. Red and black nipple tassels fluttered free, the thin cords smacking against her skin. She launched the bra into the crowd before grabbing her full breasts and jiggling them in her palms. Releasing her breasts, Sara pumped her fist in the air and danced like a madwoman to the final twenty or so seconds of a song she considered her personal anthem.

As Freddie Mercury's voice faded on the track and the

pounding guitar and drums took over, Sara danced backward toward the car. Just seconds before the song ended, she hopped onto the car's edge and fell backward into the backseat, feet straight up in the air.

When the curtain fell, the club shook with thunderous applause. Her body vibrated with the excited shouts and whistles. Breathless, she panted and touched her face. What should have been one of the proudest moments of her life was tainted with the regret of what had happened with Zel. Even now the memories of yesterday intruded. She wished she could just forget the whole ugly scene.

With her crew's help, Sara got out of the backseat and returned to her dressing room. Lucy helped her clean the body paint off her backside. While not a particularly glamorous moment for either of them, they managed to laugh about the lengths they both went to in order to provide the best show possible. As always after debuting a number, they discussed the minor changes she might make to the routine the next time she used it.

Keeping with her fifties theme for the night, Sara changed into a hip-hugging red dress with a sexy pencil skirt and pleated bust. She styled her hair into a fifties-inspired coiffure and slipped on a pair of designer pumps. Back out in the crowd, Sara plastered on her brightest smile and schmoozed. She wished BJ the very happiest birthday and even had a piece of cake.

As soon as she could, Sara slipped away unnoticed through a back exit. Her entourage of assistants, stylists and crew members stayed at the club with her blessing. They deserved a night of enjoyment for all their hard work.

But Lucy, hardworking, loyal and the best sister ever, bundled her into the backseat of a private car that whisked them away from the noisy nightspot. "You okay?"

Lucy knew everything that had happened last night. Sara had never kept anything from her sister, especially not something *that* important. The only details Sara had kept to herself concerned the manner of Lalo's death. That was a secret she would take to the grave.

Everything else had been fair game. Lucy had agreed that there was nothing good that would come from telling the rest of the family that Ramsay had shown up in Las Vegas or the way he had tried to attack her or the way Besian had made him disappear. It was better if they went home and never mentioned him at all.

"I'm fine." Feeling so incredibly alone, Sara stared out the window and watched the blur of the passing strip. Try as she might, she couldn't stop thinking about Zel. Soon, he would be climbing into that eight-sided cage for that barbaric fight. Her stomach churned at the conjured image of his bruised and battered body. If he were hurt badly, she'd just die.

It seemed ridiculous that she could care about one person so deeply after so short a time, but there it was. Her heart clenched as she realized just how much she cared about Zel. This wasn't infatuation or lust. This was something more. Something so serious she trembled with its power.

The limo rolled to a stop, and the driver climbed out but he didn't open the door. Sara glanced at her sister with confusion. Her sister looked anxious and a little guilty too. Narrowing her eyes, Sara asked, "What did you do?"

"Last night, I made some new friends," Lucy said as she

opened the flap on the leather messenger bag she carried everywhere. "Erin Markovic is pretty much the nicest woman I've ever met. She's sweet, and she cares about her husband's fighters."

Sara swallowed nervously. "And?"

"And she wanted me to give you this." Lucy handed over a legal-sized envelope.

Sara took the envelope from her sister. Curious, she squeezed together the metal brads and shook the contents of the envelope into her palm. She frowned with confusion at the pictures that fell out and into her hand. The first was a snapshot of the cutest little boy. Sara didn't even have to turn it over to identify the child. It was Zel's son, Matthias.

The next picture was a group of shabbily dressed young children ranging from toddlers to teens stood on the steps of a rundown building. Faded and chipped painted letters arched over the entrance. *St. Marko Krizin Orphanage.*

She stared at the faces of the children, noticing their haunted eyes. Upon closer inspection, they all looked a bit skinny and ever so sad. Her heart broke for the poor little creatures. She could tell by the age of the picture that it was at least thirty years old. Was one of those little boys Zel?

The final photo was a snapshot of Zel, Ivan, Alexei and some other men, all of them brawny fighter types, in their workout clothes. They were sweaty and laughing. It was a brotherhood of men who shared the same gym space.

She unfolded the note that accompanied the photos and read the handwritten message from Erin Markovic.

Zel is like my Ivan. Believe me when I say that you will never find a man more loyal or loving than Zel. Don't

let him slip through your fingers now. He fought for
you. It's time for you to fight for him.

Her gaze drifted to the VIP credentials that had fallen onto
her lap when she had given the envelope a shake. Sara swallowed hard as she realized this was one of those moments she
would look back on some day with the utmost satisfaction or
the deepest regret. It struck her quite suddenly there wasn't
really a decision to be made. She wanted Zel. She wanted to
apologize and make things right.

"I'm supposed to tell you that if you aren't going those
photos need to be returned to Besian tonight. Erin kind of
borrowed them from Zel's hotel room."

Sara put the phots back in the envelope. "I'll give them
back to Zel myself."

Lucy grinned. "Go get your man, Sara. For once in your
life, be happy."

Sara didn't hesitate. "I will be happy."

Lucy leaned over and kissed her cheek before tapping on
the car window to signal the driver. The door opened, and she
stepped out of the vehicle. Bending down, she instructed,
"Don't worry about me or the rest of the team. You go and do
your thing. I've got this."

"I love you, Lucy. Thank you."

"I love you, Sarita. Good luck!"

The door was shut, and the driver slid behind the wheel.
He glanced back at her, catching her gaze in the rearview
mirror. "You just sit tight, Miss Rubens. I've got friends
working security. We'll get you right in the fight."

"I hope so," she whispered, desperation overtaking her

body.

The next twenty minutes were the longest of her life. The driver wove in and out of the heavy traffic. Sara's eyes bugged out at some of his maneuvers. Once, they barely cleared another car's side by mere centimeters, but so long as he kept the car moving forward, she didn't care.

Antsy, Sara fidgeted with her skirt's hem and wondered what the hell she was going to say when she saw Zel. Somehow "I was wrong" just didn't seem to cut it. But it was the best she had. It would have to do.

When they neared the arena, her driver took a side street that led them to a back entrance with loading docks for vendors. The moment the limo stopped, Sara bailed from the backseat and dashed toward a pair of security guards chatting animatedly with someone hanging out near an exit door. *Besian.*

The mob boss smiled at her as she raced toward him, tottering on her too tall heels. He made a show of checking his watch. "You cut it close."

"I got her here as quickly as possible, Mr. Beciraj. Just as you instructed," her driver said.

"I appreciate it." Besian handed the driver a thick envelope. "You'll stay here until my friend and her man are ready to leave. The guards know a place you can park."

"Yes, sir." The driver happily pocketed the envelope.

Sara presented her credentials to the security guards. One of them flicked his fingers after studying them. "Follow me. I'll get you to your seats."

Bubbling with excitement and relief, Sara latched onto Besian's arm. "Thank you so much! You have no idea what this means to me."

Besian kissed the top of her head. "You'll always be one of my girls."

Her relationship with Besian would always be hard to explain to an outsider. They were friends, but more than friends. Their friendship had survived so much because they had never fallen prey to the messy romantic entanglements and sexual attraction that ruined so many of these types of relationships. It seemed oddly fitting that the man who had shown her a way to save her family ten years ago was now showing her how to save her budding romance with Zel.

They traversed a series of labyrinthine hallways and stairwells. Employees rushed along the same corridors, often shoving her out of the way in their haste to get to their destinations. Sara didn't care. She just needed to see Zel.

As they neared the arena floor, the deafening cacophony took Sara by surprise. She had never been to a fight like this and had no idea what to expect. The guard paused at an entryway onto the lowest—and seemingly most expensive—deck of seats to converse with another set of guards and an attendant of some sort. Their tickets were inspected and they were waved through.

"You're on your own now," Besian said before giving her arm an encouraging squeeze. "I'll catch up with you later tonight."

Sara nodded and followed a woman in a red vest and black slacks down a small set of stairs to an aisle seat.

Erin Markovic occupied the seat right next to hers. She looked incredible in a sexy dress with an edgy cut. The shimmery gold fabric of the pencil skirt hugged her hips and outlines her curves beautifully. The white camisole style bodice popped against her tanned skin and dark hair. Louboutin heels and gold jewelry complemented her outfit to perfection. Her smoldering eye makeup and bright red lipstick popped.

Erin smiled and gave her two quick air kisses and a hug. "It's almost time for Zel to make his entrance."

A heartbeat later, the lights dimmed and loud music blared over the speakers. Sara's heart fluttered in her chest as she glanced back in the direction Erin pointed. It made sense that Ivan's wife would have the perfect seats right along the corridor where Zel and his team would enter. She couldn't see him at first and looked toward the massive television screen mounted high above them for a better view.

Tense. Powerful. Handsome. Zel looked every bit the warrior he was. His serious gaze was focused forward on the looming black cage as he advanced down the aisle. Ivan and the rest of the coaching staff flanked their fighter, all of them in the trademark black and red clothing favored by the gym.

As Zel drew near, Sara looked away from the screen and toward the aisle. She held her breath as Zel came into view. She almost didn't want him to see her. She worried that seeing her and remembering everything that had happened last night would shake his concentration. She would never forgive herself if he got hurt because she had rattled him.

But when his gaze skipped from the cage to her face, she didn't see shock registered in his expression. The tension in his jaw relaxed, and his mouth twitched with the barest smile. His eyes were warm and hopeful as they settled on her. She smiled at him, the silent gesture begging his forgiveness and encouraging him at the same time. Zel winked at her, and Sara's heart raced with sheer joy, the pulse pounding in her ears so loud she couldn't even hear the raucous crowd surrounding them.

Dazed, she watched as Zel mounted the steps and entered the cage. While Mace worked his way down his corridor, Zel stood still and let the referee and cutman inspect him. After Mace had gone through the same routine, the emcee finished his dramatic introductions and Zel got his final moments of coaching from Ivan. The referee called both fighters to the center of the ring where they squared off as he gave his final instructions.

When the starting bell rang, Sara thought she might pass out. Her entire body felt hot and then cold as her blood pressure spiked and her heart raced to keep up with all of the adrenaline that had just been released into her blood stream. Mace swung first, and Zel evaded the massive punch, landing one of his own to Mace's ribs.

With that first trading of blows, the crowd went nuts. Sara tried to follow the fight, but it was hard. Every time Zel took a hit, her stomach lurched. Every time he landed a hit, her heart flip-flopped in her chest. Calm and cool, Erin stood next to her and watched the pair with the practiced eye of an avid sportswoman. She didn't look particularly concerned or worried so Sara decided that Zel was doing just fine. There was no need to panic.

When the bell rang to end the first round, Sara practically collapsed in her seat. She watched anxiously as Ivan got in Zel's face, wiping away the sweat and a trickle of blood on his chin with a towel. He pressed a small metal rectangle on Zel's cheek and talked to him, his expression calm but his delivery forceful. Another trainer offered Zel water. He drank a mouthful, swished it around and spit it out, all the while nodding and listening intently to whatever coaching Ivan was giving.

Too soon, Zel was on his feet again and fighting. Sara noticed that Zel seemed light on his feet and full of energy while Mace looked heavy and slower. He looked like a car about to run out of gas, surging forward but held back by an empty tank. Was he sick? Was he injured?

"He cut too much weight," Erin called over the roaring din of the crowd. "That's what you're wondering, right?" Sara nodded, and Erin said, "He needed a fight. He needed a win. His coach and the league pushed him to drop a weight class." She shook her head. "And now look at him."

Even fighting at less than one-hundred-percent, Mace was still a bruiser. His hits were nasty, and he seemed to match Zel in skills. By the time the second round ended, both men were bleeding and panting. Mace dropped like a sack of rocks onto his stool while Zel walked back calmly and sat down easily.

Again, Ivan was in his face, wiping away blood and sweat and treating the swelling while giving him pointers. Ivan seemed wholly focused on Zel, completely unaware of anything but his fighter. Some of Sara's anxiety fled at the realization that Ivan would do whatever it took to protect his men.

The massive screen above them caught her eye. The live view of the mat showed blood stains and spatter. It was a brutal reminder of the vicious combat happening right in front of her. Unable to stomach the sight, she glanced away and found herself locking eyes with Besian. He seemed pleased by the fight so far. No doubt the longer this went on, the more money he would make. If Zel's odds had stayed at the rate she had taken earlier that morning when she had placed her bet, Besian was going to make a fucking fortune tonight.

The third round began. By now Zel's face was in full bloom. His left eye was swelling shut. A gash split his left temple. He was injured, but he wasn't slowing down. If anything, he seemed to have a burst of energy as the bell clanged. He attacked Mace with his fists and took the other fighter down to the mat with a kick.

"Sweet Jesus," Sara whispered as Zel pounded Mace with his fists. Mace threw back his elbow, narrowly missing Zel's nose. When Zel leapt back, Mace clambered to his feet. They circled one another, bobbing and weaving as they waited for the next opening.

Sara glanced around helplessly. She didn't know how to read the scoreboard. Was Zel winning? How many rounds were left? How much longer would this go on? Judging the intensity of the crowd, Sara guessed the fight was in its final minutes. She closed her eyes and prayed silently. *Please let Zel win.*

A shocked gasp rocked the crowd. Sara's eyes flew open just in time to see Mace land a vicious kick to the side of Zel's head. He teetered on his feet before falling forward in what seemed to be a jaw-rattling landing. Sara nearly puked at the sight of Zel's lolling head and the blood dribbling down his mouth. The smirk on Mace's face filled her with fury.

"GET UP, ZEL!" Sara shouted manically, as if he could hear her over the din. "GET UP!"

Mace approached Zel with a predatory grin. Sara realized he meant to land the final blow. Her stomach nearly turned itself inside out as he pulled back his leg in preparation for a nasty kick. She could see the muscles flexing in his bulging thighs as Mace drew back and whipped his leg forward.

"NO!"

At the very last second, Zel leaned just far enough to the left to avoid the deadly blow. In a flash, he grabbed Mace's ankle and jerked the man off balance. Mace slammed into the mat so hard his head bounced twice. Zel was behind him in an instant, his forearm locked around Mace's head in a viselike squeeze. It was a repeat of last night. Mace flailed and clawed at Zel's forearm but to no avail.

Zel popped him once in the temple, his fist battering Mace's head like a hammer—and Mace was out.

The arena exploded as Zel gently lowered Mace to the mat and staggered to his feet. Zel thrust his gloved hands high in the air and dropped his head back, shouting his elation. Bloodied, bruised, battered—but he was a winner.

Ivan surged across the mat and wrapped his crazy huge arms around Zel, hoisting him high as they both laughed and shouted with joy. Sara's knees gave out and she crumbled into her seat. Tears of relief flooded her face. With trembling fingers, she shielded her face.

It was over.

Zel won.

Zel was safe.

And now he's free...

CHAPTER TEN

FOREHEAD AGAINST THE tile, Zel let the hot, pounding pressure of the shower ease the tension in his shoulders and neck. He felt as if he'd been hit by a semi. Every muscle in his body ached. The slightest movement sent waves of discomfort through his stomach. His med check had ruled out any severe injury, and while that knowledge pacified his usual post-fight anxiety, it didn't do much to reduce the soreness. Only the sweet taste of victory lessened the pain.

And what a victory it was!

Zel couldn't have asked for a better retirement fight. He could walk away from this life satisfied he had made his mark on the world of mixed martial arts and done his very best. Mace had rung his bell in those final seconds, but somehow Zel had managed to summon forth the last remnants of that primal energy deep within him to win it all. From this moment forward, he would hold his head high.

He switched off the shower and cautiously crossed the wet tiles. Zel snatched a towel from the bench and wound it around his waist. Grabbing another, he used it to dry his hair and wick away the moisture clinging to his upper body, his bare feet leaving heat marks on the concrete floor as he walked to his locker. As he applied his antiperspirant, Zel heard the door behind him open.

"You okay?" Ivan's voice boomed inside the cavernous locker room.

Zel cringed. "I'd feel better if you weren't shouting at me."

Ivan laughed. "This might be my last chance to yell at you. I decided to get it all out while I can."

Zel glanced over his shoulder at his longtime trainer and confidante. "Just because I'm not going to fight for you anymore doesn't mean you can't call me up to yell at me every now and then."

"Or maybe you can come back to the gym and work with me," Ivan suggested.

Zel was taken aback by the offer of employment. "Are you serious?"

Ivan shrugged. "We'll talk about it when we get back to Houston. You need some downtime to recover before you make long-term decisions, but yes. I think you would be a strong addition to our team."

"Thank you. I'll think about it." Surprised by the offer and thinking of all the possibilities, he turned back to his locker and grabbed his antiperspirant. "The warehouse had a good night."

"A very good night," Ivan agreed. "Your night is about to get better."

"Oh?"

"Sara is outside with Erin. If you want to see her—"

Zel spun around so fast he banged into his open locker door. "I want to see her."

Ivan smiled. "I'll send her in to see you." He retreated toward the door but paused. "You two need to save the makeup sex for later, okay? You have a press conference in about twenty minutes."

"I can do a lot in twenty minutes, Vanya."

Ivan's laughter echoed in the locker room. Zel gulped as anxiety invaded his belly. At the sound of the door opening and the unmistakable clack of heels against the concrete, Zel's heart raced with anticipation.

He had forgiven her the moment he had walked out of her hotel room last night. She had been scared—both for herself and for him. Sending him away, ending things so abruptly, had been her way of protecting him. She had been trying to shield him from all the trouble that seemed to follow her.

At first glance, her decision was a selfish one, but later, on reflection, he had seen it as a sign of selflessness. She was willing to give up a chance at happiness to keep him safe. That made him want her—love her—all the more.

Like that first night, she took his breath away. She was so beautiful and that dress highlighted every luscious inch of her gorgeous body. He was proud of her for coming back, for being brave enough to make things right.

The sight of her puffy red eyes made his chest tighten. "You've been crying."

She nodded.

"For me?"

Sara's lower lip trembled. "Your face…"

Zel barely heard her distressed whisper. He self-consciously touched his swollen left eye. "It's fine. The swelling will be gone in a few days. You'll see." She didn't look convinced. He fought for the right words. "You came."

Tears dripped down her cheeks. "Yes." Sara stepped forward hesitantly and then stopped. "I'm so sorry, Zel. You were right, and I was wrong. I never should have sent you away. You and I do have something special, but I got scared. I started thinking about all my mistakes and all the ways I've hurt people—"

Zel quickly crossed the distance between them. He gently cupped her face and kissed her more passionately than he ever had. "I don't care," he murmured against her soft, sweet mouth. "You're here now. That's all that matters."

Sara's shoulders sagged with relief as he tightly hugged her to his chest. For a long time they simply embraced, content with just being together again. Eventually Sara pulled back and looked up at him. "So what happens now?"

"Now? I go to a press conference and then I get something to eat. After that, we go back to my room or yours, and we sleep."

"Just sleep?"

He shot her an amused smile. "I'm no good after a fight, baby. Give me a few days to recover and then I'll rock your fucking world."

Sara laughed and tenderly kissed his jaw. "And what happens after you recover?"

He shrugged. "I have no idea."

She bit her lower lip before asking, "Come with me?"

He wasn't quite sure what she was asking. "Where?"

"Everywhere," Sara said. "Travel with me. You have a passport?"

"Yes." He didn't like to admit it but it needed to be said right up front. "I'm broke, Sara. I don't have two nickels to rub together."

"You do now."

He narrowed his eyes with suspicion. "What does that

mean?"

"It means I put some action on your fight with Besian. You earned that money protecting me." She lovingly touched the cut on his neck. "It's yours. It's your starting over money."

"Sara…" He had never taken a dime from anyone. He wasn't sure he wanted to start out their relationship with a gift like that, but he sensed this was non-negotiable for her. There were no strings attached that he could see, and he didn't think she would ever hold it against him. He would probably end up spending it all on her anyway…

"I have shows lined up all across the US, Canada and Japan for the next three months. After that, I'm free. We can do anything you want. We can go back to Houston. We can go live in Europe. We can rent a beach house in Turks and Caicos and live off rum and whatever you catch and cook." Clearly nervous that he would reject her, she repeated, "If you want to come with me, I mean."

Zel had never seen her look quite so vulnerable. His heart swelled with love for her. Like him, she had seen so much in her life and deserved a fresh, clean start.

For the first time in years, he was filled with hope. With Sara's help, he would write the next chapter of his life.

Smiling, he interlaced their fingers and touched his forehead to hers. "Wherever you go, I'll be right there beside you, Sara."

The End.

For Free Reads that continue each couple's story and for new release and sales announcements, please sign up for my newsletter.
http://eepurl.com/sX-z1

Also by Roxie Rivera

Her Russian Protector
Ivan

Dimitri

Yuri

Nikolai

Sergei

Sergei 2

Nikolai 2

Alexei

Kostya – Coming 2016

Ivan 2 – 2016

Danila – 2016

Fighting Connollys
In Kelly's Corner

In Jack's Arms

In Finn's Heart

Debt Collection
Collateral

Collateral 2 – Coming 2016

Past Due – Coming 2016

Paid in Full – 2017

Down Payment – 2017

Final Installment – 2017

About the Author

A *New York Times* and *USA Today* bestselling author, I like to write super sexy romances and scorching hot erotica. I live in Texas on five acres with my red-bearded Viking husband, our sweet, mischievous little girl and two crazy Great Danes.

You can find me online at www.roxierivera.com.

Made in the USA
Las Vegas, NV
24 October 2021

32971545R00079